PENGUIN
BY THE SA

Esther David is an artist, critic, professor of art and a columnist for the Ahmedabad editions of *The Times of India* and the *Indian Express*. Her first novel, *The Walled City*, a story of three generations of Indian Jewish women was published to wide acclaim.

BY THE
SABARMATI

Esther David

PENGUIN BOOKS

PENGUIN BOOKS
Published by the Penguin Group
Penguin Books India Pvt. Ltd, 7th Floor, Infinity Tower C, DLF Cyber City, Gurgaon 122 002, Haryana, India
Penguin Group (USA) Inc., 375 Hudson Street, New York, New York 10014, USA
Penguin Group (Canada), 90 Eglinton Avenue East, Suite 700, Toronto, Ontario, M4P 2Y3, Canada
Penguin Books Ltd, 80 Strand, London WC2R 0RL, England
Penguin Ireland, 25 St Stephen's Green, Dublin 2, Ireland (a division of Penguin Books Ltd)
Penguin Group (Australia), 707 Collins Street, Melbourne, Victoria 3008, Australia
Penguin Group (NZ), 67 Apollo Drive, Rosedale, Auckland 0632, New Zealand
Penguin Books (South Africa) (Pty) Ltd, Block D, Rosebank Office Park, 181 Jan Smuts Avenue, Parktown North, Johannesburg 2193, South Africa

Penguin Books Ltd, Registered Offices: 80 Strand, London WC2R 0RL, England

First published by Penguin Books India 1999

Copyright © Esther David 1999

The illustration on the title page is by Pushpa Rajaram; all other illustrations are by the author

All rights reserved

10 9 8 7 6 5 4 3 2

Reprinted in 2014

ISBN 9780140278439

Typeset in Galliard by SÜRYA, New Delhi
Printed at Repro India Ltd., Navi Mumbai

A PENGUIN RANDOM HOUSE COMPANY

To Lila Jivaji Thakore, Laxmi, Pushpa Rajaram, Sairabanu Pathan, Faiz Mohmed, Hasmukh Mistry and Langha Ahmedbhai Savabhai.

Contents

Contents

Prologue

These are the stories of women in, as far as I could make it possible, their own voices. When I think of them, the picture that comes to my mind is of women dancing around an image of Goddess Durga on a starry Navratri night. The eyes of the goddess follow the dancers as their eyes follow hers, creating a lake of eyes. Shimmering in the light of their own reflections, sparkling in their finery, the women conceal the reality of their secret pain in the mystery of their kajal-filled eyes.

Writing about them was like dancing with them on such a night, and being aware, as we moved in rhythm, of the subtle shades of happiness and unhappiness that imbue our lives.

And as I listened to their stories, one lesson I learnt was that when women hold hands, they experience strength, a feeling of well-being and togetherness which helps them fight their battles. I have, therefore, placed myself in the circle of their experience, which I have tried to understand in the first person, like a first story, my story—your story.

Father

It was the coldest day of the year when Mulji came to ask for Maghi's hand in marriage. In gratitude, Deva looked up at the sky and thanked God. A square cloth was between him and the sky. It was the only home they had. That day, the cloth looked like a marriage canopy.

Deva sat where the cloth was held closest to the ground. His ancient shirt was irreparably torn, and the loincloth did not help keep away the cold. He shaded his eyes with his cracked palm and watched Maghi, who stood the cold better than him. She had wrapped her sari around her shoulders as she sat beside the open mud stove on which she was cooking rice in a clay pot. Deva studied her dark sad eyes and noticed the specks of dust on her face. Beautiful daughter, thought Deva, if only some young man had asked for your hand, instead of Mulji.

And he thought about the distant village where he had grown vegetables. The drought had brought them to Ahmedabad—homeless, braving the sun and poverty.

In between, Maghi had grown up into a beautiful young woman. Her mother had died soon after her birth and she had had to learn the laws of survival from an early age. Deva could not work for long hours as a labourer because he had tuberculosis, so she took up work as a servant in the houses around their shack near Anjali cinema.

Mulji is much older than Maghi, thought Deva with a sinking heart. In fact he was as old as Deva, but Maghi had agreed to the marriage. For a moment Deva slipped into a daydream in which he saw Maghi dressed in gold and brocade, like the bride of a young prince who had a two-storied palace with a cement roof. A real house which had doors, windows, beds, blankets, an iron stove and a storeroom full of grain. Deva consoled himself that Mulji would treat Maghi like a queen. He would have preferred to give her a proper marriage ceremony, but Mulji was a widower, and so according to custom he came with a coconut and a thousand rupees which he gave Deva as the bride price.

It was then that Maghi realized that her father had sold her to Mulji. As she left for her new home with Mulji in an autorickshaw, she had a strong impulse to ask the driver to turn back towards home. But she could not gather the courage to do something like that; instead she sat withdrawn in her corner till they reached his house.

Maghi was received warmly by the women of Mulji's family. They teased the young bride, as they showered her with rice. Through her veil Maghi watched the precious grain being thrown at her. Helplessly she watched it mix in the dust and she thought of Deva, alone and hungry. She had touched his feet in farewell as he had sat in his corner. The rice that mixed in the dust would have been enough to make a meal for him. Fortunately her face was covered with her sari and none of the women could see her tears.

Mulji left soon after for his evening drink and Maghi was left alone in the small brick house. She closed the door, and for the first time in years she had a bath with warm water. Then she wore a new yellow and green floral sari which Mulji had given her along with a gold necklace and bangles, silver anklets and armlets which had designs of fishes and scorpions.

Bathed and dressed, she felt pleasantly relaxed as she examined the jewellery. She did not want to think that they had once belonged to Mulji's first wife. Maghi experienced a sense of security between the four walls of the house. She also had a variety of vegetables and fish to make a full meal after countless hungry years. She felt strangely indebted to her father.

That night, she felt a certain happiness as she fed Mulji and his son Kesha who appeared to be as old as she was. From behind her veil she saw that he was watching her young hands and there was an expression of scorn on his face. Maghi decided to keep away from him.

After the meal she felt a sudden surge of well-being, then immediately felt sick, thinking of her old father sleeping in the open ground near Anjali cinema. Later, as she snuggled into the quilt, she had a strong desire to run to him with a blanket and a plate of food. Instead she lay quiescent in Mulji's tight embrace.

That was the coldest night of the year. Many people died that night. Deva was one of them.

The Full Moon

My parents told me that to gain a new life, I must
discard the other life which does not belong to me. So
my head was pushed into the water. The water went into
my eyes and nose and I felt as though I was drowning
and close to death. The hands, big and strong, smelling
of tobacco, kept pushing me back into the water. I was
helpless as I was dashed into the water again and again
till I felt the blood flowing from my head when I hit a
stone.

I was sure they were going to kill me. Were they
murderers? If they were, why did the police stand around
the pond eating hot jalebees?

For a moment my head was lifted from the water and I saw an orange full moon within the circle of the four heads around me. Together, they looked like a four-headed demonic mask. I still remember the detail of each head as it bent over me. I was amazed that I could smell the camels standing nearby.

The face of each man was different, yet they seemed to resemble one another in their greed. The thin one had high cheekbones, buck teeth, oily hair, and a small thin moustache, as though someone had drawn a line over his teeth. The older one had a long grey beard like a holy man's, and lips stained red with paan juice. The small one was bald. He had thick lips and kohl-filled eyes, which looked like two holes in his head. The fat one had a square flat face with kind eyes and hair growing from his ears and two enormous teeth hanging over his lips. His spittle was dribbling down his chin, but before it could fall on me, my head was again ducked back into the water.

I was delirious when I screamed 'Let me go', and immediately they released me from the torture, because they thought it was Mina speaking to them and returning to her own world.

Mina had been my best friend; we had grown up together. She had died two years back but my parents said her dissatisfied spirit was living in my body.

I was dropped on the cement paving around the pond like a wet piece of cloth. Half dazed, I could hear screams around me, as many more people like me were dashed into the water. I could sense that there were more women than men.

I could not breathe and wanted them to leave me alone. But that was not the end. They were pulling at my clothes and jewellery. It was a ritual that followed the drowning. There was nothing I could do, and I could see my mother hiding her face with the end of her sari. I could feel one of the men trying to remove the scorpion-shaped toe ring which Mina had given me. The ring seemed to sting the man but he did not say anything. For a moment I was terrified that he would cut off my toe just to take the ring.

After the looting ceremony, they left with my sari, necklace, rings and anklets. Carefully the white-haired saint had unscrewed my gold nose ring and taken it. As he breathed into my face, I felt like throwing up. I would have liked Mina to claw his face but they had driven her away. Mother was wiping me with the end of her sari and thanking Goddess Ganga for saving me from Mina's spirit.

Mother was wearing a white and red tie-and-dye sari. The red spots on it reminded me of the blood on Mina's dead body when they brought her back to her mother's house.

I wanted to look back at the pond of screaming humanity but Mother held my arms and Father held the back of my neck so that I would not look back. They said that if I looked backwards, Mina would follow me again.

At the bus station, a cup of tea revived me. My eyes were burning when I looked up at the orange full moon. It was the same moon which had shone on Mina's wedding day. But when they brought her corpse back home it was a moonless night, and a trickle of blood was flowing from her head, just like the blood that had flowed from mine. I felt the blood on my hands and wanted to scream in the same way that I had been screaming for the last two years. I decided not to when I looked up at the stony faces of my parents. The ordeal had been too much for them. I was afraid to scream, as we were still in Pushkar and my parents would have again taken me back for the drowning ceremony, assuming that Mina was still within me.

I felt a tear trickle down my cheek as I thought that I had lost Mina for ever. My mother was crying into her tea, all the while cursing Mina for ruining us. Then she tore an end of her sari and tied a bandage on my forehead.

But for me, it is not easy to forget Mina. We lived in the same street. We went to the same school near Bhadra Fort. We lived in small houses of wood, all crammed together, in tiny shaded streets. The street was our universe with the cows, the cyclists and the bent old women going to the temple. Sometimes we played inside the house or read stories to each other. But the game we liked best was playing 'house' with little brass kitchenware. We cooked and ate imaginary dishes made with green mangoes and neem leaves. We played husband and wife by turns, wearing Mother's saris and Father's kurtas.

In a way we believed that we were married to each other. We even celebrated our wedding day by exchanging garlands we had made with jasmine flowers, and with our pocket money we bought a bar of chocolate. Our faces were smeared with melting chocolate but we refused to tell our mothers that we had bought it with our own money for a special occasion. We were spanked, but did not reveal our secret.

Our life was like a dream till we turned fifteen and our mothers said they were looking for grooms for us. Mina's father stopped her from going to school and soon she was engaged to be married to a boy she had seen only once. I was luckier, as I was dark and not as beautiful as Mina. It was hard to find a match for me so my father said that I could finish school and attract a groom with a good education.

As I studied for my exams, Mina sat next to me and read my textbooks. She wore half-saris over long skirts and said that she would rather be my wife than marry a man she did not know. She did not like him as he did not resemble her favourite film star. As the day of her wedding came closer, I was sad that I would not see her every day, for her fiancé's house was on the other side of the river. Gradually I saw less of Mina as her mother kept her busy with the wedding preparations.

One evening, she came to see me and whispered that she wanted to tell me a secret. So we went to sit on the parapet of my terrace, as we used to before her engagement. She appeared greatly disturbed, because her fiancé had taken her to see a film that evening, and in the darkness he had tried to touch her breasts. As she cried in my arms, I felt afraid for Mina. We were still in our teens, somewhere between childhood and a distant adult life that frightened us.

The day Mina was married, I was like one mesmerized with the beat of the drums and Mina's tears. I thought she would never stop crying. The women said it was natural for a girl to cry on her wedding day.

Then I did not see Mina for a year. My mother told me that while I was at school, she came occasionally to see her family, but always with her sister-in-law.

On one such visit I had a holiday and Mina's mother called out to me to come meet her. Mina looked very thin and sad and did not smile like she used to. I assumed it was because of her sister-in-law's presence. She sat like a guest in her mother's house. We could not talk but when she was leaving, we embraced and she quickly slipped a small piece of paper in my palm. It said that I should inform her parents that if they did not give the rest of the dowry as soon as possible, her in-laws would kill her.

When I gave the message to her mother, I was shocked to find that they already knew about Mina's situation. But they were helpless in the matter; they could neither cope up with the demands of her in-laws, nor bring her back home, as after marriage a girl's place was in her husband's house.

Then, after six months, Mina's dead body came back to the street we had played in. They said she had committed suicide. We knew that they had killed her, and the letter that Mina had written to me was useless. The women said it was her good fortune that she had died a married woman.

I could not stop thinking that if Mina had not been married, we would have been preparing for our school exams. All I could see was her sari with the bloodstains, and the marks of violence on her body when we dressed her in her bridal finery for the funeral. After that, I always saw myself dressed like a bride on my funeral day, and I would end up screaming and calling out to Mina. This happened often. Mina's dead body stayed in my memory, and sometimes I felt that I was Mina. Often they had to tie me to my bed or else I ran out into the street, thinking that she was waiting for me.

Gradually our neighbours were convinced that Mina's tortured soul was living in my body. As for me, I was gripped by a fear of marriage. Anyway, nobody wanted a mad daughter-in-law, and I was saved from Mina's fate.

My mother tried everything to cure me—talismans,

holy water, lemons thrown at crossroads. The family doctor suggested a psychiatrist but my father refused, saying that I was not mad and that somehow he had to get rid of Mina from my body. A friend advised my father to take me to Pushkar in Rajasthan, which is how we went there.

For fear of being drowned again, I decided not to mention Mina and went back to study for a teachers' training programme. I was tired of Mina, tired of myself.

But my peace was short-lived. One evening I was on the terrace looking at the moon rising over the rooftops and thinking about Mina. My mother came upstairs and sat down beside me. She talked of this and that for a while, then took my hand in hers and in a persuasive voice said that I had a marriage proposal from Mina's husband.

Suddenly, I could hear Mina laughing within me. I felt myself slipping from the terrace and hitting the ground where we used to play. Around me there was a strange fragrance of blood, chocolates and jasmine flowers.

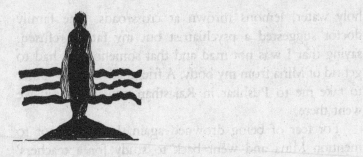

Zhunzhun

As long as I live, I can never forget that fateful morning when Zhunzhun took my sisters to their death. They had come to Bahiyal for my engagement ceremony. And now for the rest of my days I will have the memory of their shrouds and the shadow of Zhunzhun buried in his bag of salt. When we lost them, it rained the way it rarely does, and it is my misfortune that I am alive to tell you this story.

Zhunzhun was our favourite lamb. When he was born, it was decided that as he had all the elements that make a perfect animal, he would be the ideal qurbani. But I cried and did not eat for four days till Father agreed not to sacrifice the lamb. Pleased, I tied a brass bell around the lamb's neck and got his name inscribed on it at the bartanwalla uncle's shop. I decided to name him exactly like the sound of his bell as he moved. Zhunzhun soon became the centre of our life, although Father kept cursing me, saying he would not be able to sacrifice a good animal and could not afford to buy another one, what after getting seven daughters married and preparing for the eighth—me, that is.

To keep my Zhunzhun I told Father that I would work in the fields of Kazimian as a labourer and help him buy another animal with what I earned. And my sisters, when they came to visit us, also fell in love with Zhunzhun. After my engagement ceremony, they stayed back and worked with me in the fields, so that we could all earn a sizeable amount to buy another dumba, another sacrificial animal.

Every morning, Mother packed our rotlas with green chillies, onions and jaggery in a piece of cloth as we left for the fields. My sisters had informed their in-laws that they would only return to their respective houses after Id. There were some rumblings in their houses, but Zhunzhun had hypnotized my sisters with his liquid eyes and they said that they would solve their domestic problems only after Id. My mother cursed me for my eccentricities, which she said would only bring ill upon the house. And strangely, so it did happen. Although I will never accept that it was because of Zhunzhun I lost my sisters. For me, the swollen river was responsible for all that happened. On that day she was like a demon as she gushed through our little village of Bahiyal. She devoured everything that came in her way. And her first victim was Zhunzhun.

The river took him without warning. Perhaps he was

fated to be a sacrifice and was the incarnation of the holy
one who had appeared when Prophet Ibrahim was about
to behead his son at Allah's demand. Who was I to stop
the hand of God? But then, he also took seven of us along
with him. Perhaps because we all loved him so much and
he, in turn, loved us, we were all destined to go with him.
I should have been the one to follow him, but
Mehmudabibi saved me.

That night it was raining heavily and not knowing
what to do after dinner, we sat and embroidered our
dupattas for some time. Then we applied mehendi on
each other's palms. The hotter the blood of the person
putting mehendi, the better the colour, and Hazra always
beat us at that. The colour of her mehendi was such a
deep orange that it looked like blood. When we had
washed the green paste from our palms and admired each
other's designs and colour, I had the bright idea of giving
Zhunzhun a splash of colour. Mother objected and said
that one only decorated a dumba with mehendi, and now
that Zhunzhun was no longer one, it was not auspicious
to colour him for no reason at all. But we always silenced
Mother with our arguments, and she always regretted the
day she had sent us to school. We always knew more than
her. Now, of course, I listen carefully to whatever Mother
says.

That night, we applied some of the leftover paste on
Zhunzhun. For a moment we felt we had made a mistake,
as he looked ugly with the thick green dabs all over him.
Then, after we had washed the green mehendi from his
wool, we decided to give him a proper scrub. Mother
warned us that he would catch a cold, as it was raining
outside. So we heated up some water on the kerosene
stove and gave him a good scrub with soap and warm

water. Poor Zhunzhun bore it all patiently, though I am sure he would have preferred to be left alone. He tolerated us because he loved us.

Once he had been washed and dried with an old dupatta he looked gorgeous with the bright orange dots, lines, circles, a sun, a crescent moon, a pipal leaf, a lotus and a scorpion that Hazra had painted on his rump to ward off the evil eye. In fact, in the brightness of his colour he beat Hazra, because the patterns seemed to shine on him like stars on a full moon night. His colour was such a deep red that for a second I shivered with fear, as I thought of the blood that I had seen flow from the dumbas of the past. I brushed aside such thoughts and to further reassure myself, said in a loud, nervous voice that Zhunzhun looked as if he was caught in a thicket of roses.

Hazra's eyes became serious and she said, 'You mean just a bush of roses, or a thicket like the one Prophet Ibrahim saw on the day of his son's sacrifice, with the animal caught in it?' The Prophet had eventually sacrificed it, instead of his son. She looked so serious when she spoke that I was scared and repeated that he looked like a chaddar of roses, to which again Hazra protested and said that I was talking about graveyards and thorns. So I quickly embraced her and said, 'Well, Zhunzhun just looks like a bouquet of roses—without thorns.' Only then was Hazra satisfied and obliged me with a thin smile. I did not know then that she was pregnant, or that her in-laws had forced her to undergo a sonography—they could not wait to know whether she was carrying a girl or a boy. The result showed that it was a girl, and her mother-in-law was insistent that Hazra have an abortion. To this Hazra did not agree, as she did not want to kill the baby girl growing within her. That was one of the reasons why

Hazra had stayed back with us, on the pretext of Zhunzhun. Her elder sister-in-law whispered this story to my mother on the day of the funeral.

That night, when it was raining heavily, the gates of the canal flowing near our house were opened for the Narmada to flow easily. The unleashed river brought in a lot of silt and by the time we got up in the morning, Bahiyal was flooded. In panic, Father opened the door, and as he did so, Zhunzhun rushed out before Mother could stop him.

This was Zhunzhun's normal routine. As soon as we opened the door, he would rush out and go to the river to join the rest of his family, who would be grazing on the fresh grass growing on the slope. Usually I tied him to the charpoy leg and he would run out only when I released him. But that night I had been careless and had forgotten to tie him. As he ran out he did not know that Father had not yet released the other animals from their shed. When Father saw him splashing and running in the water, he ran after him to save him.

Father could not chase an obviously excited Zhunzhun, who was playing in the water with high leaps and bounds. It was Hazra who first heard Father's cries and ran after him to save Zhunzhun. But Zhunzhun was heading straight for the mad river. Hazra could run faster than Father, but the water and the slush was so bad that she slipped and fell twice. She was soaking wet and there was mud all over her; then she felt something hot like blood flowing between her legs, but she had to save Zhunzhun from sure death.

She felt relieved to see Zhunzhun standing calmly at the water's edge and wondering where all the soft green grass had disappeared. She eased her pace because she did not want to scare him, and walked carefully and slowly so that she would be able catch him unawares.

When she reached him, Zhunzhun had already started descending the slippery slope of the river. Perhaps he was thirsty after all the running around. In a panic, Hazra started hurrying, but she was walking against the flow and her salwar was slowing her down. She stopped to hitch up her salwar and in the process lost her balance and fell. She felt a gush of wetness between her thighs, and sobs rose in her chest. Yet she stood up and managed to hold on to Zhunzhun's rump where she had painted the scorpion. But it seemed to have the sting of death, because Zhunzhun started slipping with the silt on the slope, taking Hazra with him. If she had let him go, perhaps she could have saved herself. But no, all she wanted to do was save Zhunzhun, she did not care for her life any more.

By then Father had raised an alarm and my eldest sister Miraj was the first to run towards the river to help Hazra. Miraj had long hair and was on the heavy side. She planted herself on the edge and held on to Hazra's kurta in the wild hope that she would be able to save them. Miraj screamed at Hazra and told her to hold Zhunzhun with one hand and give her the other. But Hazra just could not manage to free her other hand as Zhunzhun was slipping from her grasp. Tearfully she looked at Miraj, who knew that they were both helpless against nature's fury. At that moment, she could not help repeating the word helpless to herself—'Helpless, just like me.'

Miraj had been married for ten years but was yet to bear a child. Her in-laws blamed her, although the lady doctor at the general hospital had told her that she was normal and that her husband should have a check-up. But her husband Mustafa refused, saying that she was insulting his manhood. Since then—this was seven years ago—he had never spoken to her. Miraj suffered silently, having buried all her maternal instincts in her womb, which she always compared to a grave. She never told us about her sorrows. With us, she always laughed and joked as though she were the happiest woman on earth.

Then, as Sartaj, my middle sister, reached the scene, right in front of her eyes a wave swept over them and like a chain-link, Zhunzhun was swept away into the water with Hazra and Miraj holding on to him and each other. And Sartaj, tormented by the nightly rape by her brother-in-law, just jumped into the water without a thought. She was a good swimmer, but it was difficult to swim against the current, where the layers of sticky mud seemed to drag her down, and all she could do was curse her destiny. The last time her husband Sultan was back from Dubai for a short holiday, she had tried to broach the subject, but he had beaten her and almost throttled her for slinging mud on his brother, whom he said he loved more than he did her. How could she make such an allegation when his brother looked after her and their three children in his absence?

As she swam, the heaviness of her heart merged with the heaviness of the muddy water, and she knew that something larger than nature was about to devour them all.

When my other sister Salma reached the river, she saw Sartaj following Miraj, Hazra and Zhunzhun. Always a little nervous, Salma just stood there screaming hysterically. 'Come back—come back,' she kept calling, as if she was calling out to her husband Karim. Night after night she slept alone and frightened, while he was with the woman next door. While screaming she lost her balance, slipped into the water, and was swept away for ever.

Roshan was younger than Hazra and she saw Salma fall to her death. She had been running breathlessly and missed her by perhaps an inch. She slid down in the silt and tried to save Salma, whom she could see drowning just a metre away. Roshan could not grasp her and followed her into the river. As she swam up to her and held her shoulder, she got the strange impression that Salma was refusing help. Roshan did not want to die, because she was very happy with Ahmed. They loved each other passionately. Roshan left Salma and tried to come back to the shore, but by then the swirling water was dragging her towards Zhunzhun and Roshan's screams for help were useless.

Sakina had heard Roshan's screams, and level-headed that she was, she kept away from the slope and ran along the river, screaming and telling her sisters to let Zhunzhun go and come out of the water. 'Why,' she screamed, 'why do you want to follow the dumba?' As soon as she had said that, she realized that Razia was running alongside and scolding her for calling Zhunzhun a dumba. 'He is not a dumba any more,' said Razia, 'we have saved him from the knife, and now we have to save him and our sisters from the river.' Instead of keeping their cool, they started fighting and the hot-headed Sakina pushed Razia into the river. They had always hated each other, as they had both wanted to marry Rahim. Sakina had never forgiven Razia for being the one to marry Rahim while she was married to Jabbar, whom she hated with all her heart.

Aghast, Sakina saw Razia was drowning. She jumped into the water and dragged her to the edge of the river. But they could not find a foothold on the slope, and at that very moment when Sakina forgave Razia, the strong current pulled them into the belly of the river.

I could not hear anything as I was fast asleep, and the machine used for pumping out the water was making so much noise that nobody in the village could hear my sisters' screams for help. The cursed pump was in any case of no use because the river had become a huge snake of mud and silt.

Then Mother woke me up to go and see what was happening, because everybody seemed to be going to the river and nobody was returning. As I ran, I met Father halfway, crying and screaming. I could only understand that he was going to get some men for help. I stepped on a stone and hurt my foot. As I ran, I could feel the blood spreading over my toe rings, but I ignored the pain and continued running.

When I reached the river there was no sign of my sisters. Far away, I could see Zhunzhun's dead body floating upside down. So I just jumped into the river to look for my sisters. In a second my feet hit the muddy bottom of the river and I began to choke. As I tried to come up for air, a strong hand caught my elbow and dragged me to the bank.

Later, when I gained consciousness, I was amongst the shrouds of my sisters. I was told that Mehmudabibi, the insane beggar who always sat at the water's edge, had saved me. I did not want to live any more, all I wanted to do was to run to the river and drown myself. But Mother had tied me to the string cot saying that I had to live for her.

But, day after day, as I sit in our empty courtyard, I hold myself responsible for the death of my sisters. And I think: God created the universe in seven days, but took away my sisters in just one day, and that one day came in the form of a dumba called Zhunzhun . . .

Tent of Bones

After the riots, when I had lost my house and belongings, Madinabi let me stay in her broken-down hut in the Gupta Nagar slums. Till then I did not know what it meant to live in a house which was as rickety as an old bullock—the sort which were regularly sold to the butcher next door. They always looked like tents which were held in place by the bones which jutted out from their bodies. I spent all my afternoons watching them, as they resembled Madinabi's tumbledown house which I had made liveable with some broken bricks and clay. The jamat had been very generous with donations of utensils, blankets and mattresses, so I had everything, although I had lost all that I had inherited from my mother.

Living in the slum was no easy matter. There was dirt and slush all around, and I had to walk a long distance to fill water from Julekhabibi's hand pump. But it was even more difficult to go further to the toilets of the municipal school, which we could use in the mornings.

I did not realize that a house would become my nemesis till I almost became homeless. Before that I had the beautiful memory of home in the municipal quarters. That is when I had my mother Fatma and brother Ayub with me. I was pampered by both—all day long I read the Koran, or helped my mother with the cooking. The idyllic situation came to an end when they accepted a matrimonial offer from my distant aunt Faridakhala who had seen me at a wedding. It was decided that I would be married to her nephew Usmankhan Pathan, who lived in Surat. According to her, he was the perfect match for me. My innocent brother had agreed without bothering to check on the prospective groom. He had assumed that Faridakhala would never be wrong in her match-making.

I dreamt of love, but I was also frightened, as I had never known any man besides my own brother. My father had died when I was two. To start a house with a young man—that is how my mother had described to me the process of marriage; so I thought of a small house with a garden, where I would sing love songs with my husband, just like my favourite heroine Madhubala, whom my friends said I resembled.

When I got married, I was shocked to see an ugly black man with pockmarks and a big moustache. Usman was the opposite of all that I had imagined him to be. There was no purity of religion or beauty of life in his ways or words. He had a foul mouth, and curses flowed with every sentence that he spoke. He had cheated us, as in the presence of my brother he behaved like a gentleman and won over my mother by affectionately referring to her as Ammijan.

My face burnt with shame and anger when I realized that he was uncouth and ill-mannered. Face to face with the reality of my life, I stopped dreaming. There was nothing left in our relationship even before it began. For me, Usman was evil, as he did all that was taboo in our religion. Every single night he came home drunk and smoked innumerable bidis, till our small room in Popatbhai Ni Chali started smelling like a tobacco factory. My brother had given his house to us as a wedding present. When our nikah was arranged, Usman had been jobless. So my brother, who was a city-bus driver, found him work through his friend Rahimbhai, who worked as a ticket checker at the Ahmedabad railway station. All day long Usman worked as a railway linesman, and spent hours on his trolley.

My brother Ayubbhai had decided to get married only after he had arranged for my wedding. Although I was unhappy and angry with his choice I kept silent, as I knew that both my mother and brother loved me and whatever they did for me was perhaps for my own good. But I did not know that I would lose them only a year after my wedding. My brother died in a road accident, and when my mother saw his dead body, she said 'Kya hua?' and with her mouth still open she fell down dead with a massive heart attack. By the time I was informed and I rushed there, I had to face two mayyats, instead of one. I never came out of the shock.

After the two deaths I expected Usman to change his ways, but he did not. In the second year of our marriage, when I was recovering from a miscarriage, he brought a young woman to our house. Her face was covered with a shiny red dupatta, and my premonition came true when Usman told me casually that he had married Jetun that morning and I would have to live with her like an elder sister.

For the first time in my life, I raged like a wild tigress and told him to leave the house for ever. I threw out all his belongings and sent Madinabi's son to call the maulvi. All I wanted was a divorce. Much to my surprise, Usman gave it to me easily. I realized I had walked into his trap.

All day long, as I sit watching the old cattle awaiting death, I wonder at my short-lived marriage. It is an unsolved riddle. Why did Usman marry me, and why did he leave me? What was wrong with me? Then I console myself with the thought that I had never liked him from the moment I had seen him, so it was good that he had gone away so easily. But after such a bad experience I dreaded marriage and decided to live alone for the rest of my days. I had the house, I did odd jobs for Madinabi and taught the Koran to children. I just managed to survive. Now the riots had brought me to this slum.

One night I heard someone banging on my wall. I was terrified, as I imagined the worst. Perhaps another riot had started and I would again lose my house. The wall was already shaky and I was afraid that it would collapse and I would have nowhere to go. The banging continued, and when there was no answer to my *Kaun hai*? I opened a window and tried to locate the source of the sound. In the dark I made out two horns and a bag of bones. Somebody who wanted to sell a bullock had tied the animal near my house, and it was rubbing its body against my wall.

Relieved that it was only a bullock, I tried to sleep, but it was impossible. I worried that the bullock would break down the shaky wall and by next morning I would be homeless. But nothing like that happened.

In the morning I went to Isubhai kasai and requested him to shift the animal elsewhere as I was afraid that it would break my house. He only laughed and said, 'Ever heard of a bullock knocking down a house?' Everybody sitting there started laughing at me. I was so embarrassed that I hid my face in my dupatta and returned home to cry behind closed doors.

For some reason the bullock stayed there longer than I expected, and day after day I spent a lot of time cleaning up the place around him. It was useless complaining about this to Isubhai, as I was sure he would make another joke at my expense. Instead, I made good use of the dung by mixing chikni mitti into it and plastering the angan and walls of my hut with a circular okdi, which gave it a presentable appearance. That night, my house felt more like a home with my handiwork. But like all my pleasures even this one was short-lived. The next day, when I came back from Madinabi's house, I was shocked to see a big gaping hole in the wall, exactly below the poster of Kaaba. I just sat down and stared at it. Now where was I to find the money to repair it? I cursed the damned animal which had made my life miserable. Then, to seal the hole in the wall, I started moving a packing case which I used as a shelf. As I was doing so, I felt that someone was watching me. Terrified, I turned around and saw two watery eyes staring at me from a tent of bones—it was the bullock.

For the first time, I felt the hardened knot of grief within me melting into something warm, a feeling akin to love—a feeling I had known with my mother and brother. The eyes of the animal moved me, as I knew that he was fated to die—just because he was useless. Perhaps we had a lot in common. I picked up the bunch of palak which I had just bought, and offered it to him . . .

The Charpoy

Even after her death, sometimes he felt as though she was sleeping on the charpoy, which was covered with the quilt she had made from her old saris. Now, he slept alone and invariably his eyes rested on the sari she had left on the hook over the charpoy. It was a deep indigo with a red border. How many times, he would sigh, they had fought over the sari. She had worn it so often that he had tired of it. He knew it as well as he had known her. The texture and the colour were so familiar to him that during the year of her death, sometimes his mind played strange tricks on him and he saw her walking around the house in the indigo sari. The house still carried the imprint of her presence. Though he missed having her around, doing little things for her, he had never expected to miss seeing her wear that sari.

When he opened the suitcase in which she had kept her clothes, he saw that she had a bagful of saris. When he went through them, he could smell the mothballs. The discoloured lines in the folds of the saris showed that she had never worn them. He was afraid to unfold the saris for fear of tearing them, so he left them as they were, and wondered what to do with them. If he had died before her, she would have found solutions for problems like these. He had never discussed subjects like death with her because he had assumed that he would die before her, and she would be there for ever.

But death had come suddenly. That afternoon, after her bath, she had hung the indigo sari on the hook and changed into a bright pink sari with blue flowers. She was tying her hair when she fell on the charpoy with a sudden cardiac arrest. He had never expected death to come so suddenly, and even after days passed by he had not had the courage to even put away her slippers which stayed waiting for her under the bed. Sometimes he would stare at the grey impression of her feet on them, feel the curve of her foot. The slippers gave him hope, they made him feel she would return and slip her feet into them at any moment.

It was the same with her saris. Every time his son and daughter-in-law came to visit him with their two children, he stopped himself from broaching the subject of her saris. He wanted to cling on to all her belongings as he felt her presence around them.

Without her, the evenings were the most difficult. During the day he kept himself busy at the primary school where he taught Geography, but as night approached he became restless for her and always had this strange feeling that she would open the door and enter the house. But this miracle never happened, so he opened the suitcase and went through her saris wondering why she had never worn any of them. There were twenty saris in nylon, polyester, silk and cotton, in pastel colours like strawberry pink, aubergine, misty grey, leaf green, sunset orange, brick red, chocolate brown and tomato red. None of the saris were plain, they all had a floral design or some traditional motif. Each one was a Diwali gift which she had preserved carefully. Even with his limited earnings, he religiously bought a sari for her and a pant piece for himself every Diwali. To please him, she wore the sari on Diwali. After that, he never saw it again. It was only now he realized that he had never bought a sari of her choice. Yet she had never said anything, as she knew that the choice of the sari depended on his finances, and she respected his need for privacy in such matters.

He remembered that the only time she had insisted on buying a sari of her choice was when they had gone shopping for their son's wedding. When he suggested that she buy a heavy green zari sari full of designs and motifs, her face froze. She would rather buy the plain sky blue silk sari with a simple gold border, she said. He remembered that after her death, all his daughter-in-law had asked for was to keep the sari. Perhaps, he thought, women understood each other better. When she had taken the sari, she had remarked that Ba always liked blues.

Watching the deep blue evening sky, he realized that his wife had always preferred plain blues, but the fool that he was, he had bought all the colours she had disliked. It was obvious that she hated floral saris and had kept the ones he bought for her locked in the old brown suitcase, untouched. Now how had the plain indigo come to her? He never bought khadi or handloom for her, though it was plain as daylight that she preferred coarse textiles. The indigo sari became a mystery as it hung over his head, and he pondered over it for no reason at all.

Was it symbolic of the only secret between them, or were there more? Slowly the sari became an obsession with him, and he discovered that it had a nice warm feeling. So even after he had opened the tin trunk and chosen a quilt and aired it for the onset of winter, he always had the sari under it, closer to his body. Now, it was no longer boring. It was sensuous and mysterious.

One evening, as he sat on the veranda overlooking the dry bed of the Sabarmati, watching a grey cloud of cranes flying over the house and across the full moon rising on the horizon, he shivered with a deep longing for her and covered himself with her sari. Tears flowed down his cheeks and suddenly he felt that his fingers were entwined with hers. The feeling was eerie, and in fear he threw the sari on the floor, but in the dim evening light he saw it still hanging from his hand, almost as though she was sitting next to him. Frightened, he stood up and realized that a loose thread was caught in his shirt button. Relieved, he removed it and threw it on the charpoy.

Then, he started a new game with the sari, pulling and knotting the loose threads. He found that the threads came off easily. This activity became very interesting for him. It filled his evenings like never before. The strings were like different parts of their life, and as he pulled each string, there was a memory or an incident attached to it. Things forgotten or suppressed resurfaced and he was brimming with all that he had experienced with her. He was amazed how insignificant incidents now became larger than life. It always happened to him when he opened the tiffin that came from a distant relative who catered to single people. By the time the tiffin carrier came to his house, the food was cold and it was always with a sigh that he sat down to eat, sometimes straight from the boxes. He had never imagined that one day he would be reduced to eating cold food. Gone were the days when she always had a thali of steaming hot food ready for him, while she would be roasting hot chapattis for him on the tava. He had never realized that as long as she had lived, right up to the moment of her death, she had always given him hot food, but eaten meals cold herself. And now it was his turn to eat cold meals.

When she was alive, day after day, he had eaten with his head bent over the thali; but once when she had made some hot ghee-soaked shira and their hands had touched as she passed his thali to him, he had felt a deep love for her. That was the only day that they had eaten together from the same thali, cooing like young lovers.

With such thoughts he continued picking threads from her sari. In fact, he looked forward to this activity with so much enthusiasm that it was like the time he used to wait for her to come to their charpoy after she had finished the housework. He lavished all his love on the sari. The five and a half meters of cloth had become symbolic of the span of their life.

When he had collected a good bunch of sari strings, he found that they knotted up in the same way as her hair used to when they slept together. He had also seen her weave her hair into a thin braid and that is exactly what he did with the thread. To avoid knotting, he braided the thread and then rolled it into a ball. He worked so diligently at the threads that by summer, when the mango trees were in flower and there was a strong sour fragrance in the air, he had made an indigo-red ball of thread which was the size of a mango. The sari no longer hung on the hook over the charpoy, instead he slept with it in the palm of his hand. It gave him a sensuous feeling as though he was sleeping with his hand on her breast. This turned into such an intense sensation that he became desperate for her and started contemplating the hook on the ceiling.

That summer he lay sweating on his charpoy, with a strong smell of ripe mangoes which he kept under the charpoy. The ceiling fan turned slowly, as there was something wrong with the switch and he had not bothered to get it repaired. To add to this he had sleepless nights with the mosquitoes buzzing in his ears. Till one night he took the indigo ball and tied the rope around his neck and then to the hook on the ceiling. At first he felt a suffocation, then a stifling feeling and after that, at last, he felt he had been transformed into a sarus crane flying towards its mate . . .

Homecoming

Those days my afternoons had an endless, idyllic quality. We lived in the pols of the walled city, where the houses loomed tall in the narrow lanes. The sunlight slanted in from the windows and the afternoons were cool. I would sit on the veranda of my house, cleaning grain, cutting vegetables, folding clothes, working on the embroidery of my saris or just feeding my son Sunil till my husband returned from work, announcing his arrival by ringing the bell of his bicycle.

But when my husband died in a road accident my world was shattered. He had come home early from his office where he worked as an accountant. On that particular day, I had decided to make an early dinner and was in the kitchen when I heard the tinkle of the bell. I called out to him, asking whether he had remembered to bring bananas for me to break my fast. The fast was for the goddess who is the guardian of the house. Sitting astride her camel of clay, her sequined eyes watched me as I turned him back from the door. I never forgave myself for this, as I had always received him there with a glass of water.

The sorrow has never left me. The guilt is always there. So I protected Sunil from every possible harm. When he grew up and went to school, I always told him anxiously, 'Son, come back soon.' Sometimes I stood at the door till he returned.

I could have married Maganbhai, the widower who lived opposite, and who had sent a proposal through my neighbour Kantaben. But the anxiety of bringing up Sunil was so powerful that I refused. Sunil became the centre of my life.

I knew no skills to face this new crisis with. I had kept aside the small fund I had received from Vinod's office for Sunil's education. All I knew was a little tailoring and embroidery and Mother had taught me how to use a sewing machine. That was all I had received as an inheritance after her death as the machine was of no use to my brother. I had no right over the ancestral property, neither did I receive anything from my in-laws, who said that Sunil would receive his father's share when he was eighteen. Till then I had to depend on the sewing machine.

At first I took orders to sew blouses and petticoats for the women of the pol. They also bought home-made pickles and snacks from me. When my in-laws heard about this, they objected and said that instead of choosing to become a tailor and cooking for other people, I should live with them and protect the family reputation. My new-found independence bothered them. I refused to live with them as I knew that I would have to live on their pity and eventually become their glorified servant. With tailoring, I would be able to keep my self-respect.

As I became more confident, I ventured out from the veranda to the cloth market of Dariapur—colourful and full of possibilities. I learnt to get orders for readymade clothes and slowly earned the reputation of keeping deadlines. In a couple of years I could employ another woman to help me. The work weakened my eyes and the endless hours at the machine were unbearable for my feet.

Sunil was oblivious to my struggle. He was so used to seeing me at the machine that he appeared to be blind to my troubles. He assumed that I had to do this for him and it was his right to use all that I earned. He studied, played cricket and envied his rich friends who lived on the other side of the river. He was ashamed that he lived in an old house in a dirty pol. I was shocked when he demanded things that to me appeared luxurious and beyond our means. But then I forgave the fatherless boy as he excelled in studies, and worked harder to buy him whatever he wanted.

My struggles seemed to end the day Sunil became an engineer and won a scholarship to study in America. I distributed sweets in the pol and swallowed my tears as he touched my feet to take my blessings before he left. I could barely manage to say, as always, 'Son, come back soon.'

Every year I received one letter in which Sunil said nothing about his return, nor did he send me money or

an air ticket to visit him. All he wrote was, 'I hope you
are well. Life in America is expensive, but I am fine.'

Then, as I lost hope, Sunil returned with his American
wife Susan, who seemed to tower over him. I felt no joy.
My tears were frozen and I was shocked to see that my
daughter-in-law had hair as white as mine. I had always
dreamt that Sunil would some day return and I would
arrange his wedding with Kanta's daughter Alka; small
and beautiful, with her long black braids. To my eyes,
Sunil and Susan looked ridiculous together. Yet I reconciled
to my fate. She was my daughter-in-law, and they looked
happy together.

Later Kanta told me that hair like Susan's were
supposed to be a mark of beauty in America. Susan
touched me by her efforts to please me, wearing saris,
eating meals with her hands and greeting neighbours
with a namaste.

It was Sunil who was uncomfortable in the old house
which was falling apart. I had not been able to invest time
or money in the many repairs it needed. I had always
waited for Sunil to take over his responsibilities towards
me and the house. But I could see that the house meant
nothing to him. He was restless to return to his own
house in America. Enthusiastically he showed me
photographs of his apartment, including pictures of his
bathroom.

To please him I spent hours cooking his favourite
dishes which he no longer relished. But Susan appreciated
my efforts. Sunil appeared to be blind to the fact that
Susan and I were happy together, speaking with gestures,
touches and smiles. I was hurt by Sunil's attitude and
sensed the futility of my efforts.

Our conflicts came out in the open when Susan fell

in our small and slippery broken-tiled bathroom. Although she said she was not hurt, Sunil fussed and fretted over her and I could not help but feel jealous that he had never been concerned about my feet, moving endlessly on the sewing machine or using the broken bathroom day after day.

Sunil was furious about the house and much to Susan's embarrassment decided to shift to a hotel on the other side of the river. As I watched them leave in the autorickshaw, I felt as broken as the house. Later Sunil's childhood friend Kamlesh informed me that Sunil and Susan were in Goa and that they would come to see me before they left.

After a month, one evening, as I sat on the veranda embroidering a sari, I heard an autorickshaw stop in front of the house. Sunil's step and Susan's perfume told me that they had come to see me on their way to the airport. I did not look up as Sunil bent to touch my feet and perhaps hear the words I always repeated like a broken record.

Instead, I could hear myself saying, 'Son, don't come back.'

Kurma Avatar

I have taken all this from you for far too long and have
kept quiet, but now the time has come for me to tell you
about my true feelings. When you first came to
Ahmedabad, I kept you with me as it was my duty. You
were without a job and I did not mind. My wife and I
fed you and I even gave you an allowance for your paan-
bidi. But what did you do? Did you care? No, you took
it all for granted. You behaved as if it was expected of us
to care for you. And you did nothing in the house, not
even small things like picking up your thali after you had
eaten. My wife did all your dirty work and you behaved
like a laat saheb, a guest who was doing us a favour by

staying with us.

Okay, you did not have a job. So what did you do? You got up late, and when I was having my lunch, you waited for my wife to give you your first cup of tea. I say first, because she had to make many more cups of tea as long as you lounged around the house. And while drinking your tea, did you ever speak to me? No—you were too groggy to speak. You sat in front of me, on my dining table, in my own house, and read *my* newspaper right under my nose. Now, is this fair? Even you would not allow this in your house . . .

Then you expected my wife to serve you a breakfast of either toast or batata pova, even while she was running between the kitchen and the dining room with hot chapattis for me. When she gave you your breakfast you did not even lift your head from the newspaper. Was she your maid?

When I left for work, she had to get the house cleaned, but you were like a blind person. You spread yourself in the drawing room in your vest with the newspapers around you while the maid did the sweeping. Did it never strike you that one should leave the room while it is being cleaned? My wife never complained. But once, when I had forgotten some papers for the office and returned home halfway, I was shocked to see the girl sweeping around you while you sat on the sofa like a lord. You did not even think of folding the newspapers and putting them away properly in the newspaper rack. No, I don't think you ever think about such things.

Then, you went for your bath when the children came back from school, the one time of the day which is very precious for my wife. Having finished the housework, she quietly sits down and eats with the children, after which the maid washes the dishes while she takes a short nap in front of the television. But she had to change all that, because you preferred to go for your bath just then. She had to tell the maid to come later, and had to keep the food hot for you, till you came to the table.

But do you know how self-centred you are? You took your thali and plonked yourself in front of the television, although you had seen her resting there many a times. Yet she never complained, till I saw her dozing in the veranda, and understood everything.

Your tortures did not end with that. No, you never bothered to wash the bathroom after using it, and she knows that I do not like dirty bathrooms, so every evening before starting preparations for the evening meal, she had to first wash the bathroom and then go shopping for vegetables. Did you ever tell her to take it easy, and that you would do the shopping for her? No, never. Even if you finished all the milk with your innumerable cups of tea, she never asked you to buy milk, or to pick up the teacups which were left all over the house. She did all this, while you sat playing carrom with the children. Were you such a child that you could not see the needs of a household?

And your habit of smoking, did you ever ask my wife whether she minded it or not? I never smoke, and she has always had an aversion for people who smoke in front of the children. What I am trying to say is that my wife does not like the smell of tobacco in the house. Yet she said nothing to you.

On Sundays you put a big heap of clothes for washing, and my wife had to help the maid as she refused to wash so many clothes. This I have seen with my own eyes. Why choose a day when she already has so much to do? But I kept quiet, although I felt that you should have washed and ironed your clothes yourself. Instead, I told myself, let him be, he will learn.

And did you even try to look for work? No. If it had not been for me, do you think you could have found work as a clerk at the Food Corporation? After that I expected you to be grateful, but no, my wife was even more harassed as you rarely came home on time. You made a habit of coming home late and never thought it necessary to inform her about your timings. In our house, before you came, we ate by eight and after that we watched all our favourite serials, and went to bed by nine-thirty or ten. But since you started coming home late, my wife had to wait up for you to open the door and warm up your dinner.

The night she saw you drunk, she was really upset. But she did not complain, she just informed me that she did not like it. I explained to her that it was your age. I have also done it. One feels like doing these things when one is young. I never stopped you from an occasional drink.

But you really shocked me when you went away to Surat and sent me a fax at my office, saying that you had married according to Arya Samaj rites. Let me tell you that we were deeply hurt. Why did you have to hide such a big occasion from us? So what if your wife is Assamese, it is your decision, your life. But you had the cheek to keep us out of this event and yet did not hesitate to come back to our house as if it was your own. My wife welcomed your wife in the traditional way and gave you the children's room. Do you think it gives me great pleasure to see my children sleeping in the drawing room? However, I told my wife that a young couple must have a room of their own. But it is difficult for the children, because you are not considerate enough to open the door early in the morning, so that they can take their schoolbooks or toys.

Chalo, I even overlooked that, but on the occasion of your marriage, I did expect you to have the decency to bring at least a bar of chocolate for the children. When you did not, I even forgave you that, and told my wife that you would learn all these little things when you have children of your own.

I also overlooked the fact that your wife is Assamese, and perhaps does not know our ways. On the other hand, she has grown up in Gujarat, so it is not that she does not know how we live. My wife continues to carry the burden of the house. Even this I ignore, as my wife prefers to be in charge of the house, though it is a different matter that you continue to live like our lifetime guests! I do not deny the fact that your wife helps in the house, but her contribution is like a mustard seed. But my wife is so large hearted, she takes all the whims of your wife in her stride, like entertaining your friends, wearing Punjabi dresses, eating out every weekend and going to the cinema every Sunday. We blame your age for all this, and overlook the fact that you never invite us to join you in any of your outings.

All this is nothing, however, compared to what is happening now. With all the help in the house, and the company of my wife and children, you told me that your wife was lonely and needed to keep a pet. My wife felt deeply insulted. Did she not give your wife good company, that she had to look elsewhere?

Yet, I asked my wife to swallow this insult too and bear with your wife. She comes from a faraway land, I told her, and perhaps feels lonely even when there are so many people around her. So I agreed that she could keep a pet.

But we never expected this. I would have understood if she had decided to keep a cat which comes and goes as it pleases, or a dog which is faithful to you and barks at strangers, or a goat or a cow which gives milk, even a talking parrot is all right, as it amuses the children. But your wife brought a creature that looks like a rock, yet makes soo-soo and pee-pee all over the place and cannot be trained. Its food is spread all over the house, and to add to this the whole place stinks like a gutter. With this, I have no more patience left for you or your wife. I think the time has come for you to move out, as my wife refuses to co-exist with a tortoise!

Kaddish

I saw her often at the synagogue and was always struck by her appearance: the sharp beak-like nose, high cheekbones, thin lips, and small beady eyes. Her hair was tied in a tight chignon and a loosely worn sari hid her tall but thin frame. There was a terrible look of loneliness in her face which made me keep my distance from her. Vaguely I knew that she lived all by herself in a small house in the old city of Ahmedabad. I had also heard that she had some problems, but did not know the details. In keeping with an old Jewish tradition, she was given food and clothing by those who had more than enough.

To me she looked like an old book whose pages are

stuck together by damp. Had I tried to pry open the pages, I was afraid that she would fall apart. Between the leaves, I saw shadows of a past which was best kept hidden in the book. To me, her sorrow was almost holy, like an old Hebrew scroll at the synagogue, kept behind a curtain in a vault that faced Jerusalem and the wailing wall.

Then, by chance, I came face to face with her. Someone had donated sewing machines for widows and divorcees of the Jewish community, and I was on the committee for allotment. Her form was incomplete, as she had not answered the questions regarding her income and marital status. Yet nobody discussed these points. Obviously everybody except me already knew the answers.

We decided to give her a sewing machine so that she could earn her own living. When we interviewed her in the small dusty office at the synagogue, under an old calendar of Moses receiving the Ten Commandments, she thanked us but told us that though she had applied for the sewing machine, she had no intention of using it, as she suffered from vertigo and could no longer work for long hours. The reason behind her asking for the machine was that she had planned to rent it out to the women of her area. In this way she would be able to earn enough without having to work on the machine.

I saw doubt in the eyes of Elisha and Aviv, who were on the committee with me. I knew what they were thinking. They were sure that she would take the machine and then sell it off. But I had seen the honesty in her eyes and admired her courage at speaking out the truth. Moreover, she went on to say that if we felt she was being unreasonable, we need not give her the machine. So, without consulting Elisha or Aviv, I agreed to her plan of action. As long as the machine helped her earn a living, she could have it.

After the meeting as I prepared to leave, I found her waiting to thank me. I shivered as she shook my hand. It was like holding the hand of a corpse. Hastily I withdrew my hand and agreed to meet her the following Sunday.

When I met her in my house, my heart went out to her. Apparently she only visited other Jews when they had something to give her, so she sat on the edge of the divan, as though she would run away as soon as I had given her a bag of rice and a sari. Slowly, over tea and cakes, she seemed to settle down. Just to start a conversation, I told her that she would definitely feel better if she helped other Jewish women with babysitting or catering, as she had told me that she made excellent festive delicacies. Her expressionless face suddenly seemed to crumple, and tears started flowing from her eyes. I was taken aback with the silent weeping of this woman: it was like seeing an ancient sculpture come suddenly to life. I was flustered and all I could do was sit next to her with my hand on her shoulder. Perhaps she needed to cry. So I let her weep, and the damp pages from the book of her life lay in fragments around us.

When she had washed her face and settled down again on the divan, I knew that she was willing to talk. And she did. She told me that her father had been a peon in a municipal office, and she was his fifth child. They were a family of three brothers and two sisters, and were so poor that when she was in the eighth standard she had to discontinue her studies and help her mother with her tailoring class. Her brothers continued their studies while her elder sister was hastily married to a distant cousin who worked as a clerk in Surendranagar.

She had never complained then as she wasn't good at studies, but now, in her present situation, she felt the lack of education. She was in her teens when her marriage was arranged with Mordecai, who had come to Ahmedabad as a weaving master in the Jupiter cloth mills. A fine catch, according to her father. With a certain remorse she remembered that even then, all the weddings in their family were held with the help of the Jewish community. 'We always lived on the mercy of the synagogue,' she said, 'and I still do, there is no escape for me, otherwise I shall starve to death.'

Mordecai was a good husband and she was the ideal wife. Except for the usual fights that couples have over trifles, they were happy, although she did not bear a child in their nine years of marriage. That was her biggest regret. A child would have given her a reason to live. Five years after her marriage, her father died from a heart attack and her mother died a year later in a road accident. Then her brothers Eliyahu and Elijah, who had trained as electricians, sold all that they owned and migrated to Canada. And although their father had wished it, the two brothers did not give anything to her or the other sister whose husband had found a new job in Calcutta. Since then she had never heard from any of them, and Mordecai had become the centre of her universe.

According to her, even if Mordecai was unhappy in their marriage, he had never let her know how he felt. He went about his daily business like a clock, and they attended every possible function, festival or celebration at the synagogue. As she described him, I vaguely remembered him as a dark squat man with a big head who always wore bright floral shirts. She must have been a full head taller than him, and to add to that, better looking too. When I asked her about the shirts, shyly she told me that she had always sewn them for him.

The tears started filling her eyes again as she told me that one day, just before Passover, the festival in memory of Moses and the parting of the sea, Mordecai disappeared.

That night she kept a silent vigil for him, not knowing what else to do. Perhaps he was held up at the mill; but whenever he was late, he always left a message with their neighbour Leelabahen who had a telephone. The next morning, with a heavy heart she went to his mill, where they told her that he had not shown up for a week. When she heard this, she panicked and rushed to the secretary of the synagogue, who tried to trace Mordecai and even registered a police case. For a week she was on tenterhooks, and the slightest movement at her door made her jump and rush out, certain that Mordecai was back. But he never returned.

Months later, when she was under great financial stress, she contacted his mill office to collect his arrears and insurance. Here another shock awaited her as the accounts department informed her that Mordecai had resigned and taken all that was due to him. She could not believe her ears. How could Mordecai do this to her? She told herself that Mordecai would never abandon her, as there was no reason to do so. She spent sleepless nights, thinking about the worst. Perhaps he had been murdered, or someone had kidnapped him. To clear her doubts, she borrowed a Gujarati paper from Leelabahen every single day and read the police column and crime news. She was sure that the worst had happened to Mordecai. His photograph in *Gujarat Samachar* and the television did not help either. This confirmed her worst doubts.

A year after Mordecai had disappeared, one day she was looking for their ration card, and she opened his cupboard, which till then she had hesitated to touch. In the heap of his old clothes, all his favourite flashy clothes were missing, and so was his passport. It was then that she was struck with the realization that Mordecai had cheated her. That was the day, she said, when she got her first attack of vertigo. Later her condition worsened when a distant relative, who had just returned from Israel, told her that he had seen Mordecai at a bus terminus there but he had disappeared as soon as they had recognized each other.

When she stopped talking, there was a heavy silence between us. I saw that slowly the book was closing, and the pages would remain unopened for God knows how many more years.

Later, I heard that she had become a little more active than before. She took catering orders or did odd jobs in Jewish homes. This kept her busy and sometimes when I met her at the synagogue, she seemed to look better, fast losing her forlorn appearance. She said that the vertigo attacks were also under control.

During the Jewish new year, I was told that she had been busy making traditional Jewish food for many families. For no reason at all, I felt relieved.

Then, on Rosh Hoshanah, the evening before the new year, our prayers at the synagogue were delayed by three hours. That afternoon she had died. In the morning she had complained of severe vertigo and her neighbours had admitted her to the general hospital and informed the caretaker of the synagogue. By the time some of us reached the hospital, she was dead. Everybody got busy with her burial, and only returned to the synagogue after the funeral.

That night, before ushering in the new year, the kaddish, or prayer for the dead, was read for her. I was deeply moved, as in a sense, she had nobody, but in her death the whole Jewish community was with her.

During the hurriedly read kaddish, I tried to catch her name, but somehow I could not hear the words, and as it was already very late, I left in a hurry. When I reached home, I cursed myself for never asking her, 'What is your name?'

Closed Doors

When we received the telegram informing us that Grandfather was dead, my parents rushed to Bombay for the funeral. They returned to Ahmedabad the next day itself, sad and tired—the telegram had reached ten days too late. They had gone to his grave with a chaddar of red roses. And I thought—hadn't Grandfather always lived in a grave?

Mother had some problem with him which I could never understand. She always referred to him as proud and egotistical, someone who wanted to live his life his own way and detested the idea of being dependent on either of his two daughters. When he had a stroke both the sisters had rushed to Bombay and tried to convince him to live with them by turns. He had refused. So they had made arrangements with his cook Sushila to look after him and had returned to their respective homes disheartened.

When I was nineteen and engaged to be married to Elisha, who lived in Bombay, Mother suddenly became sentimental and desired that Grandfather should bless me. Till then, I had only heard his name and had never met him. We did not have his photograph in our house and I had played games with myself trying to guess how he looked—perhaps he was fat and cuddly like a teddy bear, or he was thin and small like a sparrow, perhaps he had a huge moustache, or did he have a long beard? Did he wear a suit, a kurta, or striped pyjamas with a half-sleeved bush shirt? In more ways than one, for me he was as mysterious as the sphinx and the thought of coming face to face with him made me nervous.

After the engagement, we took a taxi to Mahim with a box of pedas. From where we stood, we could see the colourful sails of the fishing boats and smell the pungent odour of Bombay duck. We could hear the heavy traffic passing by as we stood in a tiny lane where the houses looked as if they had been hit by an earthquake. Clothes were hanging everywhere and there was a strong smell of garlic and bird droppings.

We were searching for a mezuzah and a nameplate with his name, when a man sitting on a basketful of poultry asked us if we were looking for the Yehudi gentleman. He pointed a gnarled finger towards a locked door on the second floor of a building near by.

We climbed the broken-down wooden staircase and reached the door with an ancient mezuzah on the doorpost.

Inside the room, Grandfather was perhaps listening to the sea and did not hear our knocks. He did not realize that one of his daughters was standing at his door and staring at the lock—the key of which was apparently lost. A brown goat with black patches and orange dots of mehendi was rubbing its back on the door.

By then, Father had become impatient and had pushed open a barred window, and suddenly the three of us could see him. Paralysed, he lay in bed with the saliva running down his chin. Perhaps bugs were biting him and he was trying to distract himself by listening to the sound of the waves. For more than fifteen minutes we stood watching him, then sadly Mother signalled to Father, the way she did at parties, that it was time to go. We were about to leave when we saw Sushila climbing the stairs.

Sushila was dressed in a bright green sari, her lips were red with paan and she was swaying like an elephant as she climbed the staircase. When she saw Mother, she started wiping tears from her eyes and mumbled something about having gone next door just for a minute. She then dipped her hand in her blouse and gave us the key.

When Mother unlocked the door, Grandfather looked at us blankly. He kept staring quizzically at Sushila, who introduced Mother to her own father. Obviously shaken, Mother found a rickety chair for herself and sat down with her hands folded on her knees. Her knuckles had become white with tension. Father had found a tripod for himself and not knowing what to do, he lit a cigarette while I thought that it was just right that I should sit at my grandfather's feet. As I sat there watching him, I knew that I had made a mistake. There was a strong smell of urine in the room and I decided that Grandfather needed a bath. I started feeling uncomfortable as Mother was watching me, she was worried that I would carry back bugs in my dress and at the same time wanted Grandfather to bless me on my engagement; but she did not know how to handle it as he obviously had no idea who we were.

Sushila kept on a loud chatter about our family tree, and slowly her words seemed to seep into Grandfather's blocked memory as he watched Mother with unblinking eyes. Then the tears started flowing. They gathered at the corners of his eyes and ran down to his ears. He wanted to say something, but the tears were choking him. Feeling sorry for him, I was waiting for Mother to hold him in her arms, but she did not. She sat frozen and silent.

Meanwhile Sushila was noisily pumping the kerosene stove to make tea for us and in her loud voice she was telling us that she took very good care of the old man. When she offered us the tea, I saw that Mother was looking at the chipped blue cups that had belonged to her mother's favourite tea set. I could see something like a tear touch her eyes, which she quickly wiped away with her hand.

While we were drinking tea, Sushila was sitting next to Grandfather, and lifting his head on one arm, she was forcing him to drink tea from a broken saucer. The salt from his tears mixed with the syrupy tea as he drank slowly.

When Sushila collected the teacups, Mother sat next to her father and wiped his mouth with her handkerchief, then holding his hand she placed it on my head asking him to bless me. I could see that whatever she was saying did not make sense to Grandfather. But Mother appeared satisfied that she had done her duty.

Then Father placed a cigarette on Grandfather's lips
and I saw a moment of peace pass between the men. The
cigarette changed Grandfather's mood and he looked
calm and less agitated. There was a glimmer of acceptance
in his eyes, something that had come twenty years too
late. He had always disapproved of Father. We left the
room with the smell of fish, urine, tears and the sound of
the sea. We never saw him again.

Circular Route

I left the house in a temper. The night before, they were all showing each other the gifts they had bought for Diwali. Enthusiastically, I joined in the festive mood, but gradually I realized that there was nothing for me. Among the crackers, clothes and sweets, my eyes had been searching for a small present that they might have bought for me. But there was nothing.

I could understand that my sons and their wives were too preoccupied with their own purchases from the innumerable sales, but that my husband had also not thought about me really shocked me. He was busy admiring his khadi silk kurta when I told myself, enough is enough. What did they think I was, the maidservant?

I had got the house whitewashed and cleaned, made the mathias, sev, mohanthal and farsipuri, bought the mukhvas and got everything ready for chopda-pujan and Laxmi-pujan. Every single detail had been worked out by me, down to ordering the strings of asopalav leaves, marigold flowers, diyas, and coloured powder for rangoli. Yet there was no appreciation. Everybody assumed that I was there to do all that I had been doing year after year. Without a word I left the house and took the first city-bus that stopped across the road. I was hurt that nobody loved me.

When the conductor asked me where I wanted to go, I said Kalupur. He looked surprised. Kindly he told me that I was in the wrong bus, as this one took a circular route and would take a long time to reach Kalupur. He advised me to take a bus from across the road which would take me faster to my destination. I smiled at his concern but told him that I wanted to take the longer route.

I took a window seat and stared out, still burning with anger: I thought about the lifelong efforts that I had made to give a comfortable home to my family. Was Diwali the occasion to make me realize how futile it had all been? I decided that I would leave them all. What is the use of living with people who do not appreciate you?

Perhaps I could catch a train from the Kalupur railway station and go to Bombay and look for an old peoples' home. It would be better to live with people who did not expect anything from you. Or from Kalupur I could take another bus back to Ashram Road and go to the old peoples' home there. I had passed by it many times and wondered about it. The people who lived there were either disowned, or had felt unwanted while living with their families—as I was feeling at this very moment.

It was all my mistake; I had always been dependent on my husband and sons. I had always thought about their comforts and my whole life had been spent in cooking, cleaning, shopping, filling the yearly stock of grains, making pickles, or organizing the little details that go into running a successful home. I should never have done so much.

I realized with a start that I had not even taken my bath. I was wearing my faded pink sari with the blue flowers. My hair was uncombed and I was still wearing my blue rubber slippers. Self-consciously I looked around to see whether anybody had noticed how unkempt I looked. It was perhaps the first time in my life that I had left the house in such a state, so I quickly tied my hair into a proper knot, smoothed down my sari and pulled in my feet, so that nobody could see my frayed petticoat and old chappals. What a mess, I told myself.

Try as I might, I could not take my mind off the house, so I diverted myself by looking at the brightly lit shops which were swarming with people. I spotted a trader selling bright cotton garlands for the gods and regretted that I had forgotten to buy one for Goddess Laxmi at home. For a moment I wondered whether I should get off the bus and buy one. Then I remembered that I was not going to return home that night. Why should I think about a family that did not bother to buy a gift for me?

As the bus crawled in the heavy traffic, I stared at the sari shops. Why had I always expected my husband or sons to buy saris for me? Why did I never buy anything for myself? Did I really like the pink and lavender polyester saris they bought for me? No. Instead I had always wanted to wear the traditional bandhnis.

Even as a young girl I had worn floral dresses which my father used to buy for us, all the time hating those blue and red flowers. The tragedy of my story was that even later in life nobody had ever asked me what colours I would like to wear. Every time they went shopping, they never asked, 'Ba, what do you want?' It was assumed that I liked pastels, because I was supposed to wear them at my age. I was angry with myself.

Angry, because I had no income of my own. I was educated, and even if I could no longer find a job, I should have tried to do something else. Instead, the house had been my priority. And what did I get in return? Nothing.

The bus stopped at a snacks and sweets shop, and I watched the rush of buyers. There were piles of laddus, mohanthal, pedas, sev, mathias—all the sweets that I made with competence. Why had I never thought of making a business of what I knew best? Everybody wanted my recipes. The women of my neighbourhood would have been happy to buy my pickles and snacks. They had asked me several times if I took orders and I had refused, thinking it might appear inappropriate. With a husband and two sons did I need anything? Yes, I needed to buy my own saris with my own money!

As the bus neared Kalupur, I noticed a woman of my age sitting two seats away from me. She had a two-year-old child in her lap and I was suddenly back in my house with Pinkie in my arms. The conductor rested his hand on the seat in front of me, and I saw in his watch that it was around two o'clock—the time my elder son's daughter Pinkie took a nap with me. I would start telling her a story, and then somewhere halfway we would both fall asleep. It was a warm and cuddly feeling with the fragrance of Dreamflower talc around us. I was sure Pinkie was missing me at that very moment and I could feel a wetness in my eyes.

I steeled myself with the thought that I was succumbing to emotional blackmail. Didn't Pinkie's mother know that she was free to work and go out as she pleased because I was always there for her daughter? At least for that she could have bought something for me.

Then, just before Kalupur terminus, I saw a shop selling children's clothes. Little frilly frocks were hanging in the shop, and I regretted that I had no money on me; Pinkie would have loved to have that lacy one with the big bow.

I reminded myself that I was not going back home, although I knew nobody knew how to light an oil lamp nor how to make a decent rangoli. But my mind was playing all sorts of tricks on me. I could not wipe out the thought of Pinkie waiting for me in the balcony. After her mother's Diwali vacation, there would be nobody in the house to look after her. The thought of Pinkie at the ayah's mercy sent shivers down my spine. I asked the conductor—'Which is the quickest possible route back to Shahpur?'

A Bed of Roses

One receives shocks in various forms, and one has to learn to live with them, thought Manjari. That day she had suddenly opened her father's bedroom door and found him sleeping with her husband, Dhiren.

Together, they looked strangely like a painting. Her father was wearing a white short-sleeved khadi undershirt with two pockets on the chest. In one of them he had kept his box of tobacco, which looked like a breast from a distance. His dhoti had moved up to his knees, exposing a skinny calf with soft curly hair. The blue napkin which he always kept with him covered his forehead like a sari. Her husband was wearing a sleeveless white vest over his striped pink pyjamas. To add to the effect, they were sleeping on her mother's favourite green bedsheet with the red roses, and it was obvious that in the tableau that lay unfolded in front of her eyes, her father had perhaps played the wife and Dhiren the husband—Dhiren, whom she could never make her own.

Try as she might, Manjari could not wipe out the two forms from her memory, because Dhiren was sleeping with her father in exactly the same way he slept with her. At her desk in the bank, Manjari tried to convince herself that perhaps it was an illusion, that Dhiren was consoling Kantibhai after the sudden death of her mother. Yet she could not deny the fact that her father was very fond of his intellectual son-in-law.

Till the age of thirty, she had ignored her family's attempts to get her married. They had assumed that she was still nursing an old wound. Rohit and Manjari had grown up together and everyone had assumed that they would eventually tie the knot. But that was not to be. He went away to Australia for higher studies, and never returned to Ahmedabad. Since then, she had suffered from a deep distrust of all men.

Ten years later, her father's best friend Mansukhkaka, who lived in Valsad, visited them with his son Dhiren who was then in his forties—unmarried, and an expert at computer graphics. He had recently moved to Ahmedabad. Mansukhkaka and Kantilal had secretly hatched a plot to snare Manjari and Dhiren into marriage.

As usual, Manjari had avoided showing any interest in Dhiren, and much to her relief, he also did not seem to be attracted by her plump and homely appearance. He was not exactly a hero either, for he was only a little taller than her with a square face, a receding hairline, sensuous lips, a flabby waistline and heavy legs. He disguised these flaws in his figure by wearing loose white kurta-pyjamas.

Manjari couldn't say no when her mother said she wanted to see her married, as both her brothers were settled in America and her sister was married to a businessman in Bombay. Her mother, Mridulabahen, convinced her that if she agreed to marry Dhiren they would ask him to live with them in their bungalow, where she would find it easier to adjust to her new life. But, before she took a final decision, her mother advised her to get to know him better, though, she said, Dhiren had already asked for her hand. Her arguments tempted Manjari to consider the proposal. Looking at herself in the mirror, she saw that she was not bad looking. She had round eyes which always had the look of surprise in them, small pursed lips, salt-and-pepper hair which she wore short, and a huge mole on her cheek. To add to this, the bright cotton saris she wore gave her a soft but distinguished look.

A few long walks under the evening sky and a couple of dosas at Woodlands were enough to help her make up her mind. The wedding was quickly arranged before either of them could change their minds. But at the reception an incident occurred which disturbed Manjari. Dhiren's friends from Valsad had been in a particularly boisterous mood that night, and she saw them sitting near the dais and cracking jokes. The words that hit her were—Just can't believe it. Then one of them who had come in late with a huge bouquet of pink roses, said to him with a cynical smile on his lips, 'Dhireniya, I never expected you to leave me, we had some great times, didn't we?—I just can't believe it, but anyway, all the best.' As he said that, he had given Manjari a long, meaningful look. When Manjari had asked Dhiren why his friends were so surprised that he was getting married, he had avoided her eyes and said, 'It is nothing, you know I was a confirmed bachelor, so . . .' then he had looked into her eyes and smiled reassuringly.

Dhiren moved into their house and Manjari was happy that she did not have to make any major changes in her life. In fact she liked having a companion and their evenings became lively as Dhiren always had a topic for conversation. Her father, Kantilal, was also happy to have a man in the house to take the place of his sons.

One year with her parents after her marriage was enough for Manjari. Like the rest of her friends, she wanted to set up her own house. So Kantilal offered them a flat he had bought for his elder son. Manjari was happy and she made a charming home with cane furniture, bright durries, Kutchi bedspreads, brass pots, and a small garden in the balcony. But she could not live happily ever after as Dhiren started picking at her for small things and would not contribute to the household expenses. He did not help her in the house either and they only ended up fighting. On each occasion Kantilal had to intervene and the marriage seemed to reach a dead-end. Eventually, Kantilal persuaded them to return to the bungalow.

With a heavy heart Manjari locked the house, gave the plants to the neighbours and wondered whether she would ever be able to return to make a home of her own. She realized that Dhiren was not satisfied with her company alone and needed many more people around him. Their love-life had always lacked the passion which Manjari had dreamt about, and there was something mysterious about him, which she could not fathom. When she confided her problems in her mother, a worried look had come over Mridulabahen's face and she had said, 'Late marriages are always like that.' Yet, to Manjari's surprise, once they returned to her parents' house, their marital discord seemed to melt away and they settled down into the smooth routine of the big house.

But Manjari was uncomfortable. She now felt like an outsider in the house that she had always lived in, while Dhiren behaved as though it was his own. The lack of responsibilities suited him, and whenever he was at home it was not uncommon to see him lounging with a book in their air-conditioned bedroom. There were no bills to be paid, no shopping to be done, and he turned a deaf ear to Manjari's demands that they share some expenses with her parents. So on her own Manjari paid the dhobi, bought groceries, vegetables, and clothes for herself and Dhiren while he lived like a spoilt child. He did not even buy gifts for anybody—his income was a secret.

Manjari wondered whether it was a good idea to have agreed to the marriage. Living in her parents' house, she was unable to grow as an individual or build a relationship with Dhiren. Sometimes, for six months in a row, they did not even take a walk together. Manjari craved to be alone with her husband, but whatever romantic ideas she had were crushed. She felt as though she had become the daughter-in-law of her own house and resented the fact that Dhiren had turned her into a stranger in her own home.

To hide her sorrow, Manjari kept busy by looking after the garden around the bungalow, which had taken a worn down, unkempt look. Just before the monsoons, Manjari hired Shankerbhai as the gardener and after he had cleared the dead foliage, they worked hard to have a fresh green lawn in front of the house, in time for the first showers. But then the green looked too monotonous, and Manjari added a touch of colour with bushes of red roses, so that from her window the green of the lawn appeared to have a sprinkling of red kumkum.

Once she involved herself in the garden she had so much to do that she stopped thinking about her relationship with Dhiren. The garden was the only thing in her life which kindled in her a feeling of love. To plant different saplings and see them grow gave her more pleasure than anything else; they were like the children she could never have, and she looked forward to the mornings and evenings when she could spend time with her green friends. In them she discovered a whole new world.

The year her mother died after a long illness, Kantilal had a nervous breakdown, and their life revolved around him and all his problems. But the sight of the two men together in bed came as a complete shock to Manjari. Fragments from their life lay scattered around her and now she remembered the hush-hush whispers, the snide remarks, the hidden smiles, and her own realization that her relationship with Dhiren had always lacked love and togetherness. There was something about Dhiren which everybody knew, and she had not understood.

Later that night, lying on her maroon bedspread with the black circles, Manjari consoled herself that her father could not possibly ruin his own daughter's life. She scolded herself for being over-imaginative just because she was plagued with doubts and tried to drive away the image of the two men on their bed of roses. But it stayed with her in her empty bed.

The next day she packed her bags and left. She was

going to make a home of her own in the flat where she would grow a small garden in the balcony. The big bungalow with its enormous garden was not for her; it reminded her of the green bedspread with its red roses!

Nobody Will Know
in Ahmedabad

That year Ruchi started losing her hair. Bunches of it could be seen all over the house. There was hair in the air they breathed and the food they ate, so much so that Ruchi felt she was going bald. No amount of oils, vitamins or conditioners helped. She wept over the loss of her hair, which had been very precious to her. Day after day she stood in front of the mirror and grieved at her loss. Her only solace were Rahul and Priya, who were confused by the happenings in their house, and Ruchi decided to save them from the emotional mess by returning to India. The old house would heal her. She no longer wanted to see either her parents, Bijal or Parantap. They could live in peace once she returned to India. But she would not give a divorce.

It had all started around the time Ruchi's parents started looking for grooms for their two daughters. It had been easy to find one for the feminine and graceful Ruchi, while it was very difficult to find a match for Bijal, just because she was tall like a coconut tree, according to the community match-maker. Ruchi was small, well-made and had long hair which reached her heels. Parantap had chosen her at the first meeting itself. For Ruchi's parents it was a matter of great relief.

Parantap lived in America. Ruchi was a pathologist and so it would not be difficult to find a job for her. She was trained in housekeeping and, of course, presentable. Seeing all this, Parantap did not want to look elsewhere. Anyway, he did not like the idea of looking for a girl in the traditional manner. But he had reached a point in life when he needed a wife. He earned well as an engineer in a company of repute and had all that a man would want to own in a lifetime. A girl from back home completed the picture in his mind. Ruchi would give just that special touch to make his life perfect. And she did. She was the model wife, and adjusted quickly to life in New York. She had a tremendous talent for adjusting to change.

After the first few days of homesickness, Ruchi quickly found work for herself in a small laboratory, and it was easier once she was occupied. She also found an Indian association which they visited occasionally for get-togethers. Parantap was amazed at how quickly Ruchi adapted to her new life. She stopped wearing saris and salwar-kameez; instead she looked sexy in her tight jeans and long hair which was a matter of discussion wherever they went, specially when Ruchi left it open. The only issue in her new life which bothered her was that Parantap was called Peter by his friends. She always winced at the name which turned Parantap into someone else. She kept her silence in the matter, as he obviously liked to be known as Peter. Parantap, she would whisper to herself, now why is such a name so difficult to pronounce? Is it necessary to cut short one's name and make it into something as ridiculous as Peter? But Parantap thought it was fashionable—so that was that.

Even otherwise Ruchi was a quiet person, and did not immediately give her opinion on any subject. Slowly Parantap realized that she had the capacity to bear any amount of pain or stress without protest. Sometimes this trait in Ruchi bothered Parantap, and he felt like shaking her and telling her to be more vocal. Once in a while when they had fights, he did just that—much to Ruchi's shock. Sometimes she could not figure out what was bothering him, but she was aware that between them there were frozen, unfathomable moments.

Then, in their second year of marriage, Ruchi became pregnant. It made her homesick and nervous. She decided to have her baby in India, where her mother and sister would always be beside her. She felt lonely and frightened, and only relaxed when she reached Ahmedabad for the seven-month ceremony at her in-laws' house. After that, she went back to her own house and felt good to be taken care of by the women of both houses. It was also good to be quiet when she wanted to be, and not make great efforts to speak, as she had to do with Parantap. Long

distance, Parantap was the perfect husband: he spoke to
her every Sunday morning, and faxed her a letter every
Friday night. Her parents were happy that Ruchi had a
happy married life—what more could parents want from
life, they told friends and relatives.

When Rahul was born, both families were content,
and after a three-month rest, Ruchi returned to Parantap.
With a child, things changed for the couple; their lives
revolved around Rahul.

After a few years, Ruchi became pregnant again and
the old homesickness overcame her. But this time she
could not possibly go to India for a long time, as Rahul
was in school. Yet the idea of being alone during the
pregnancy depressed her. At first she did not want to tell
Parantap, but one night, over dinner, she casually
mentioned her fears. She also told him that her family
was planning to make a trip to America to look for a
groom for Ruchi's younger sister. It was decided that she
should write to her parents asking them to come in the
last months of her pregnancy, so that she could have her
little India around her when their second child was born.

This is how Ruchi's father Shantilal, mother Urmila,
and younger sister Bijal came to live with them in their
three-bedroom apartment. Shantilal had retired a few
years back and Bijal had come on a long leave. She
worked as a marketing executive in an export house.
Urmila had always been a housewife, and happily took
over the kitchen, much to Ruchi's relief. The overactive
Rahul and her advanced pregnancy were wearing her
down, and once she had explained to them about super-
markets and subways she was happy to prepare for the
new arrival. It was a girl, whom they named Priya.

In a month, when everything had settled down,

Shantilal started his search for the ideal man for Bijal, who was then reaching her twenty-ninth birthday. Bijal was the complete opposite of Ruchi. If Ruchi was short and had long hair, Bijal was tall, wore saris, tied her hair in a thin oily braid and had an immense capacity to chatter which invariably gave Ruchi a headache. All the men Bijal had seen in India were shorter than her, and she had decided that if she married, it would be to someone taller. The prospective grooms that Shantilal and Parantap had found for her were somehow just not right for Bijal. Either they were educated and short, or tall and not as educated as she was. This put the entire family in a turmoil, and all discussion centred around Bijal and her suitors.

In fact Ruchi had started feeling uncomfortable with Bijal, who spent hours talking to her brother-in-law, while she rarely had anything to say to Parantap. Ruchi remembered that even when they were children Bijal had been a chatterbox. She shrugged it off as nothing, yet felt a quickening of her pulse when she saw them together.

To please Parantap, Bijal changed her name to Betty, and she enjoyed laughing and joking about it, calling it a Peter–Betty game, while Ruchi simmered silently. She was relieved when they returned to India. But they had filed their applications for green cards before leaving. Shantilal had decided that eventually he would find a groom for Bijal, and then they would all settle down in America. Families must stay together, he had said. Ruchi could not decide whether this was a good idea.

Back in India, Bijal found some fault or the other in the men that her father introduced her to. Disheartened, he stopped looking for grooms as word had spread in their community that Bijal was too old for the marriage market. All she could find now were divorced men or widowers. Urmilabahen wrote a long letter to Ruchi saying how worried she was about Bijal. Ruchi wrote back to her mother saying that as long as she was there, they need not worry about Bijal—she had found the right match for her. Bijal was sure to like Dr Ashish Modi when they returned for their green card.

So, during their second visit to America, Bijal met Ashish. They appeared to like one another, and saw each other for two months, as Bijal had insisted that she would like to know him better before she took any decision. She did not let anybody know that she had already decided not to marry him; she thought he was tall but fat. He also expected her to wear trousers, while she preferred saris. When she gave her verdict about Ashish, the whole family was stunned. Her reasons for not accepting Ashish were shallow. Bijal laughed at them and asked Ruchi to find her someone like Parantap. Ruchi was so embarrassed that she left the room without a word. She was aghast; Parantap was indeed taller than Bijal, and it was obvious that she was attracted to him. Besides, she also knew that Parantap preferred Bijal's chatter to her silence.

Weeks passed and while her family was still with her, Ruchi went back to work, and Bijal earned a little extra something by babysitting. She was also exploring the possibilities of importing readymade garments from India. With some shock Ruchi realized that she was stuck with them, and had no personal life left with Parantap. To add to this, he was planning to move to the suburbs and take a bigger house there. Ruchi felt upset, but decided to keep quiet, as it was useless trying to talk Parantap out of this idea. He was the one who took the decisions, without ever consulting her.

When they moved into the bigger house, Ruchi discovered that Bijal and Parantap were getting closer to each other with their Peter–Betty games, and she could do nothing about it. Finally one day she had a showdown with Parantap that brought the whole problem into the open. Grimly, Shantilal told Ruchi that Bijal was in love with Parantap. Her parents asked her to solve the problem, and for the first time Ruchi flared up, and told them that they had ruined her life. Did they expect both sisters to live in the same house with one husband?

Ruchi was even more infuriated when in the privacy of their bedroom, Parantap told her that since theirs was an arranged marriage, there had never been any love between them. All he felt for her was a deep sense of duty. But what he felt for Bijal was more akin to love and they had a lot to give each other. With Ruchi he hardly had anything to say. Ruchi, furious, asked him what was expected of her. Parantap had no answer, but from his eyes Ruchi could see that instead of the daily fights, it would have been just perfect for him if both sisters could live with him under one roof. Ruchi was even more shocked when she realized that her parents too wanted her to come to terms with this, as Bijal was not likely to find a husband for herself. Shaken, Ruchi told them to return to India, where Bijal could live as an old maid for the rest of her life. Urmilabahen almost agreed, but Bijal refused to return; she wanted Parantap at any cost.

Defeated, Ruchi buried herself in her work and in looking after the children. The days passed by and Parantap and Bijal got closer to each other. Ruchi could do nothing. That was when she started losing her hair. The thick long hair which had evoked such admiration from everyone now lay in bunches all over the house.

Ruchi was almost at her wits' end till one afternoon, she took a good look at herself in the mirror and aghast by the sad, worn-out image, decided to take matters into her own hand. If her family did not want to return to India, she would. She also got herself an appointment with the hairdresser and asked her for a very short haircut. The woman shivered as she held the scissors, and asked her to think again, it was no joke cutting off such beautiful long hair. Ruchi remained unmoved. When she heard the scissors moving in her hair, and saw the long tresses on the floor, she felt tears sting her eyes. But when she finally stepped out into the sunshine, she felt better and stronger. Somehow, the long hair had got her entangled into a strange family drama, and she wanted to get it out of her way.

That night, after she had tucked in the children, she shocked the family with her smart short hair, and firmly told her mother not to cry over it. She was unusually lively when she told them about her decision to return to India with the children. They all fell upon her, saying she could not do that as people back home would ask questions. 'You cannot possibly do something so drastic,' they said, 'people will immediately understand that there is some problem between you and Bijal, and we will never be able to return home.' At the end of the arguments, Ruchi was defeated, and she had to lay down her last weapon.

Snared in the family blackmail, Ruchi decided to move out of her bedroom and make a place for herself in the children's room. In her efforts at making a corner for herself, she noticed that the design of the house was such that she could easily partition it in two by locking one door. So one afternoon, when nobody was at home,

Ruchi quickly took whatever she needed and locked the connecting door. She also made sure that a small wicket gate would serve as a separate entrance to her house. She explained to the children that as she was having problems with their father and the rest of the family, they would live in this part of the house, away from the rest. But they could see their papa whenever they wanted to.

Then Ruchi left a note on their dining table, saying that Bijal could have Parantap, on the condition that Ruchi would keep one part of the house as her own, and they need not bother her or see her. Rahul and Priya would visit their father whenever he was free, but he need not enter her part of the house to meet them. While her parents could see her by appointment, and according to her wishes, she would not return to India. With this final solution, she wrote that Peter and Betty would be safe in America and nobody would ever know in Ahmedabad!

Moment of Madness

On the other side of the river, among the concrete structures of modern Ahmedabad where bins of garbage and bright T-shirts are reflected in the glass windows of the smart shops, one can often see a madwoman with the beggars, balloon sellers and the lone flute seller.

When I first saw this woman, I was in a restaurant. I could see her from the big glass window framed with plastic creepers. The food stuck in my throat as I watched her. A naked child played around her. With a shock I realized that she was Shridevi. I recognized her by the eyes which resembled broken green glass. From a distance she looked blind because of the colour of her eyes.

She was rubbing sand in her hair and she was almost naked as she sat on the pavement, a small loincloth tied around her waist. Although dirty, she still looked beautiful.

With a searing pain I remembered her story. She was the young bride of my friend Savitri's brother, Anil, who had been a perfectionist in the matter of choosing a bride for himself. He believed in horoscopes and planets, but he also wanted beauty and it was never easy to find a combination of both.

As a rule, when he went to see a girl, the prospective bride was presented in a brocade sari with a trayful of home-made sweets and snacks. This confirmed the fact that she was not lame. And when she answered questions, the groom's family knew that she was also not dumb.

Anil boasted that he had rejected fifty girls before he had given his consent to marry Shridevi. He saw her simplicity, the beautiful eyes, her skills at cooking and did not want to see her horoscope. The family arranged the marriage in a month.

Within a couple of weeks of the wedding Savitri said something had happened to Shridevi. She was depressed and kept sitting in a corner. She refused to do anything. She did not cook, she did not smile, and refused to sleep in Anil's room. Naturally, Anil was angry. He wanted a divorce and regretted that he had not had her horoscope examined. But the family did not want him to divorce his wife. What would people say? Instead, they subjected Shridevi to medical tests, to long sessions with psychiatrists and medical advice of all sorts. But she refused to cooperate with the doctors.

Once, when I had gone over to Savitri's house to pick up a book, Shridevi was being taken to a godman and Savitri asked me if I would like to accompany them. I agreed out of curiosity. When I smiled at Shridevi, she had a strange gleam in her eyes. She seemed to be acting out a scene from a play, the script of which was known only to herself.

The godman sat with closed eyes and Shridevi sat staring in front of him. To me she looked like an angry goddess. If she had the power, she would have burnt them all to ashes. According to ritual, Shridevi's head was covered with a new unstitched cloth and Savitri offered the godman a huge basket of fruit and a hundred-rupee note for his services.

The man chanted, and Shridevi seemed to smile as the man asked the evil spirit to leave her. Then, loudly, he started narrating how the spirit had taken over Shridevi's mind. He said that the spirit had seen Shridevi's pregnant mother one evening, and followed her into the house where it made a place for itself. When Shridevi was born, this spirit kicked her mother down the stairs and killed her. It then entered the newborn child from the umbilical cord and stayed there. The child was dying, but was saved by her grandmother. When Shridevi was married, her husband became the spirit's competitor and it wanted to spoil her married life.

Hearing this Shridevi started laughing hysterically. The family bowed before the godman and begged him for deliverance. They looked at Shridevi with fear and anger in their eyes and Savitri whispered in my ear, 'What shall we do? She has killed her own mother. She is evil.'

I was shocked that Savitri, my friend, should believe in such things. But in spite of all her education and the years spent doing social work, she was suddenly afraid. So I offered to help—I would speak to Shridevi. After a week I invited her for tea. At first she was suspicious of me. But slowly she relaxed and told me her story.

She said, 'On the day of the wedding, my niece Shiela came from Bombay. She is a lively fun-loving prankster. In contrast I am shy and quiet. I take time to open up. At the wedding reception I noticed that my husband was attracted to her, but as I was myself preoccupied with thoughts of my new life, I did not pay much attention to his behaviour. After the marriage rites, when we entered our bridal chamber, Anil did not seem to be in a mood for love or romance as I had expected him to be. I was naturally shy and confused. Anyway, I knew very little about such matters and I had met him only once, so I just sat on the bed with all the jewellery and the heavy brocade sari, waiting for him to make the first move. It was very hot, and I would have liked to change into something light. The sari, necklaces and garlands were suffocating me . . . But he just sat by the window and smoked cigarette after cigarette. At last he turned to look at me and his eyes seemed to soften. At that very moment there was a knock on the door. It was my niece Shiela. She did not look at me, but spoke directly to my husband and asked him, "What were you saying about your hair? I could not hear you at the reception." "Ah yes," he said. "Why don't you do something about my hair, it's turning grey." He was laughing.

'Shiela sat by him on the bed and he rested his head on her knee. As she touched his hair, I walked out, and spent the night on the balcony. I could not shout at them and defame my own family. There was nothing I could do but suffer. I was tortured with the thought that on the very threshold of our married life, my husband had betrayed me. And that too with my own niece.

'The next morning I asked Shiela if she would like to

marry my husband, as I was willing to give him a divorce. To this she replied abruptly that she had a steady boyfriend in Bombay. She was sorry about what had happened and begged my forgiveness. She cried bitterly on my shoulder and said, "It was a moment of madness." I gently pushed her head back, and that afternoon she left for Bombay.

'Since then I am in great pain. I wish Shiela had agreed to marry Anil. Now there is nothing I can do. If I tell my in-laws they will never believe me.'

True enough, when I forced Shridevi to tell Savitri the truth, she did not believe her; instead she blamed her for making up a story about her brother.

After some time Shridevi took her father's advice and mended matters with her husband. She could not return home because her father depended on her brother who had a family of four, and Shridevi had no qualifications to earn a living. She was compelled to adjust to her husband and his family. Then I lost touch with Savitri and her family.

Years later when I met Savitri again, she told me that her brother had divorced Shridevi on the grounds of mental instability and infertility and had remarried Shridevi's niece, Sheila, whose horoscope had matched his. The only problem was that Sheila could not conceive either, because of a defect in her womb. But did that matter, asked Savitri.

With Savitri's words reverberating in my mind I dropped my shawl on the half-naked and mad Shridevi playing with her child on the pavement. I wondered whether she had been raped. Was it Anil's child conceived before the divorce; or was it the evil spirit?

Ahindro

It all started when Vesti became a widow and the villagers suspected her of the evil eye. They said that things went wrong because of her. With all the worries that followed Manga's death, Vesti had aged in a week. They had no relatives and Vesti was left all alone, with nobody to turn to. They had survived on the vegetables they had grown on their little patch of land. So, even before the mourning period was over, Vesti had gone back to work, as she knew that if she did not, she would starve. That was when the women of her street turned against her and taunted her by saying, 'What a woman you are, going to work without a cover on your head and mixing with the traders of Godhra just to sell your vegetables. Filling your stomach seems to be more important to you than the eleven-day ceremony of your husband!'

Vesti did not answer them; instead she stared back. There was something so ferocious in her eyes that the women had turned away and called her a witch.

In Shehra, a tiny village in the Panchmahals, Manga and Vesti had always had a hard time surviving. They lived hand to mouth, and during the drought they had survived on a boiled mixture of roots. After Manga's death what did they expect her to live on?

She had always been an outsider. She belonged to Vandar which, like Shehra, was a village in the interiors of the forest. One needed strong feet to walk the hilly terrain and reach these villages. The tribals who lived there had to walk long distances to reach Godhra where they looked for work. Before she married Manga, Vesti too used to go there every day. Her father had a good harvest of leafy vegetables but as he was lame, it was the sure-footed Vesti who went to Godhra, sold their yield and returned the same day. So she was always in a hurry, and that was how Manga met her. They sold their vegetables to the same trader, and Vesti always irritated Manga by insisting that she finish her deal before anybody else. When he had fought with her for being too overbearing, she had started screaming at him that she was from Vandar and wanted to get back before sundown. Manga had understood her problem and struck up a friendship with her. Sometimes, he even walked her up to a turning from where the dirt road to Vandar was safe.

When they met the next day Vesti would be anxious to know whether his return to Shehra had been safe because she knew that whenever he accompanied her, it was sure to be midnight by the time he reached his village. She always worried that she would not see him again as either a panther could have devoured him or he could have died of snakebite on his way back—it was an encounter with a panther that had left her father lame. Manga was flattered by her concern and knew that at last he had found the right woman in Vesti.

But, somehow, he was always tongue-tied when it came to expressing his desires. To be on the safe side, he had found out from her that she had been a child bride. But when she reached puberty and her in-laws were asked to accept her, they informed her father that they were helpless in the matter, as their son, a ballboy at the Devgadhbaria sports centre, would not accept her unless he had seen her.

When he came to Vandar, Vesti had taken one look at him and known that he would never accept her. He was wearing a bright yellow shirt over dark, shiny trousers under which she could see his red socks and dirty second-hand tennis shoes. As long as he stayed there, he never once took off his rainbow-tinted sunglasses. Vesti stared uncomfortably at her own reflection in them. The distorted image of her face in the rainbow made her feel ugly and unfit for marriage. As Vesti had expected, they were called by the panch, who declared that her in-laws wanted a divorce because their son did not like her. Vesti had already prepared her father for the worst by telling him to accept the decision of her in-laws. If her husband did not like her, it was better not to continue with the marriage. It was obvious that he thought she wouldn't fit in with his lifestyle.

Vesti had accepted her fate; she would now live the

life of a divorcee without ever knowing the meaning of marriage. She took upon herself the hard task of dealing with traders and walking up to Godhra and back. Then, after meeting Manga, she had started dreaming. She knew that Manga was an orphan and had no close relatives to arrange for his wedding. But she did not know how to tell her father or Manga that she wished to start a family with him. So she resolved to offer seven clay horses as a votive offering to her ancestors during Holi if Manga received the message of her heart.

Then, at the Holi fair, in a medley of sounds and riot of colours, it happened. They were sitting in the giant wheel when Manga asked her if she would share his house with him. According to tribal custom he could not marry a divorcee, he had to just give a kumkum-stained coconut, a rupee and a piece of jaggery to her father. She accepted his proposal atop the giant wheel.

After years Vesti had dressed up in a bright red sari which she had wound tightly around her slim body. She wore a saffron-coloured puff-sleeved blouse to go with the sari. Her face was the colour of copper, her hands shone with bangles of all colours and earrings covered her entire ear with all sorts of designs. Around her neck she wore long silver and bead chains and heavy anklets on her slim legs. Manga could not take his eyes off her black kohl-filled eyes, the tattoo marks on her cheeks, the shining nose ring and the silver on her teeth. If he could, he would have taken Vesti as his bride at that very moment.

And Vesti, watching him shyly, thought that they looked good together. He was not wearing his usual green loincloth and grey baniyan, but was dressed in a colourful pink dhoti over an embroidered green bandi.

He was wearing silver anklets and bracelets on his wrists, and the silver chains around his neck were swinging over his ebony chest. On his head he had tied a purple cloth.

Vesti stopped herself from touching him. She understood the look in Manga's eyes and knew that before they got carried away by desire, they would have to take her father's permission. She told Manga exactly where he was—playing the dhol in a circle of young men dancing the raas with long sticks. They waited for her father to finish one round, after which Manga stepped into the circle, danced with the others and then stood next to Vesti's father. While he was still playing the dhol, Manga told him that he wanted to marry his daughter. The old man lost his balance for a moment as he suddenly shifted from one foot to the other, and after taking a long look at the young man, he nodded yes. Tears streaming down his eyes, he started playing a louder and faster beat—and through the whirl of dancers moving with their sticks, when his eyes met his daughter's, he was smiling.

That afternoon, under the tamarind tree, Vesti's father accepted the traditional offering of a coconut from Manga and after they had exchanged marigold garlands and touched his feet, he declared them man and wife. It was a simple, touching ceremony under a bright afternoon sky, and it brought tears to Vesti's eyes.

Manga bought for Vesti bright green bangles, as a symbol of their new life. She got his name tattooed on her arm, around which she asked the tattoo-maker to draw birds and flowers. Then she asked for a scorpion to ward off the evil spirits, and added some more dots on her legs and one special beauty mark on her chin.

She bought seven clay horses from the Poshina potter, and that evening, with her father leading the way playing on his drum, she went with some women from Vandar to the Ahindro or mountain god's dwelling place under a huge banyan tree. Vesti placed her offerings under it and thanked the gods for giving her Manga; with folded hands she prayed for Ahindro's protection against evil and animal. This is how Manga and Vesti started their new life in Shehra and they were happy till Manga was struck down with malaria.

It first started with a bodyache. Vesti walked on his back and pressed all the points which hurt him, but that did not help. He had fever with a splitting headache, and the doctor was far away in Godhra. All she could do was send for the vaid who asked her to make a concoction with some roots; but that too did not help. So Vesti asked Bhura from the neighbouring plot to call her father as she did not know what to do. She wanted to take Manga to Godhra and needed another shoulder to carry him there. She would have to climb down from the hills to reach the dirt road, and only then reach the main road—from where they would perhaps catch a state transport bus or a tempo to the Godhra General Hospital.

It appeared impossible, but when her father arrived, she did manage to reach Manga to the hospital. By then he was in a bad way and even though the doctors tried hard to save him, Manga died in a week. Taking Manga's body back to Shehar would have been a nightmare, so she decided with her father to give him a lonely funeral in the Godhra municipal crematorium. She had always asked Ahindro to protect Manga from evil and animal, but she had never imagined that a mosquito would take his life!

With Manga's ashes in a clay pot, Vesti returned to

Shehar and immersed them in the little rivulet that flowed next to her house. All alone in her hut, in the dim glow of the lantern, night after night she cried, but continued to work in her plot of land during the day. She began to sense a buzz of suspicion around her. She could not understand what was the matter, but knew that everybody in the village held her responsible for Manga's death. As a divorcee, the villagers had always considered her to be evil and a bad influence. The women had always stayed away from her, but Vesti had never bothered as she was happy with Manga and he had always been there to protect her. Now suddenly alone and the target of vicious allegations, Vesti felt afraid. When Bhura next door also came down with malaria she went to visit him. As it happened, he died that very evening, and all fingers were pointed at her.

Since then, she did not know which way to look or whom to turn to. She could not return to her father's house either. Her sisters-in-law always referred to her as the one-with-the-black-face, and according to her father, they did not want Vesti's shadow to fall upon their children. She was left with the small piece of land as a solace. Despite his bad foot, her father walked long distances to help her sell her vegetables, and Vesti felt relieved to see him for an hour every day.

But then one incident was to follow another in quick succession, and Vesti was so confused that she did not know what to do. A comment she made about the bright brick colour of Soma Vira's cow resulted, they said, in the animal's milk drying up. Then Mangi started losing her hair, just because Vesti had appreciated her long braid. That week, it also happened that one night hundreds of flying foxes invaded the mahua trees and ate up all the fruit, and the men could not make their local brew. To add to this, the crops failed, and the village bhuva held Vesti responsible for the misfortune that had come upon them. That night she understood that the village elders would brand her as a witch because she had refused to give her land to the sarpanch.

A witch—the word itself sent shivers down her spine, as she remembered how Rasika and Kapuri had been stoned to death. Again she prayed to the gods Ahindro and Govaldev, and vowed that she would offer a himaryo— a seated horse—to the sanctuary of the gods if she could ever get out alive from Shehar. Before sunrise, she ran away from Shehar, sliding down the unused hilly terrain behind the village. She wanted to avoid the dirt road and did not know where this would lead her, yet she kept on going. The more she thought about the bhuva and the people of Shehar, the more she prayed to Ahindro to help her. When she had covered quite a distance from Shehar, she hit upon a track, and the footmarks there made her feel better. Suddenly, she heard the sound of hooves, and she turned around to see a man on a horse. As he came closer she was relieved to see her reflection in the rainbow-coloured sunglasses of the rider. But she did not want to take his help nor show that she had recognized him, and kept on walking as though nothing had happened. But much to her amazement, the man stopped in front of her, took off his glasses, and asked her, 'Are you Vesti?'

Pushpa

When I was twelve years old, I was married on a full moon night. I was half asleep as Father dragged me around the marriage fire while I could hear the women singing. When I was being sent away to my husband's house, Mother cried bitterly. I tried to keep awake by lifting the veil that covered my face, but the women pulled it down and told me to keep it there. They told me never to lift it, unless I was alone in a room. I was suffocating in the heavy silk.

We left that same night for my in-laws' house in a bullock cart. I fell asleep with the movement of the cart and the sound of the bells tied around the animal's neck.

I do not know who carried me into the house, and who made me stand in the doorway as my mother-in-law welcomed me into my new home. Yet I do remember that my sari was tied to my husband's scarf and it was very difficult to walk together.

Then I was led to a room where there was a string cot decorated with flowers. I was so tired that I just lay down there and slept, as I assumed that this was the end of the ceremony. But that was not to be. I woke up with a start when my husband tried to remove my clothes. I was so afraid that I held on to my sari. He saw the fear in my eyes and let me be, as he was himself a boy, just a year older than me.

I hated my veil, as I could never lift it and see things properly, and it always enveloped me in a haze. So I entertained myself by using the colour of my sari like a transparent glass. When I looked through it everything in my world was tinted with different colours. It was a game I played with myself. Sometimes, green fields appeared orange, the moon looked purple and the sun could be either grey-brown or black. Even faces changed colours, like the colours of a rainbow. The face that never changed colour, however, was that of my mother, it was always there in a flood of white tears.

But my husband was colourless. The moment I heard his footsteps, I closed my eyes. Then one day, serving him his dinner in a peacock-blue sari, I saw through my veil that he was tall and beautiful just like our god Krishna. That was the day I felt the first stirrings of emotion for the boy who slept with me every night.

Slowly, as we grew up together, it was easy to fall in love, and I waited for our beautiful nights, when we would be alone in our room and I could uncover my face to look at him. In three years we had two children and we were happy in the fresh air of the fields, where there was plenty of everything. But this was not to last. Soon we were to drown in a river of blood.

One afternoon, as I was sitting on the veranda and nursing my daughter, I felt my milk turning sour, as I heard the painful screams of my husband. They brought him home wrapped in a bloodstained cloth. I wanted to tear my veil and look at him, but could not, as all the elders of the village were standing around him. With tears streaming down my cheeks, I watched him through the tint of my rose-pink sari, and saw an endless dark red smudge turning into what seemed to be a big black cloud in front of my eyes. He had lost his arm in the mustard oil press machine, and seemed to be floating in a pool of blood. He was rushed to the hospital by my father-in-law in an ambulance.

During the three months that my husband stayed in the hospital, I saw him only once. That was when my mother-in-law took me to the hospital with the other women of our family. Through my veil I saw that he looked thin and wasted and had lost his colour. He looked sad and incomplete without his arm. I could not touch him in the presence of the other women.

When he came back home, he seemed to have turned grey; he felt he had lost his manliness with his arm. He tried to cover up his loss with the empty sleeve of his shirt. Defeated, he sat on the veranda day after day, watching the fields with empty eyes. As for me, all the colours of the rainbow disappeared from my veil. Only two colours dominated my life now—a patch of red, with a black border.

As my husband could not work in the fields, the

family would not help us, and soon we lost our share in the family income. That was when our maternal uncle came from Ahmedabad to visit us and when we told him about our plight, he invited us to try our luck in the big city. I felt a deep black fear enveloping me, as we packed our belongings in a little tin trunk. I did not know what the future held for us.

In Ahmedabad, we lived in a small hut by the Sabarmati. I woke up early in the morning and wrapped sweet peppermints in cellophane paper which my husband sold at the bus terminus. We could buy food only when he returned with whatever he had earned, and we ate the leftovers the next morning. The dirty slum on the river bank seemed so far away from the fresh fields, and I seemed to have lost all those colours which I used to see through my veil. But sometimes I saw a pool of white colour from the veil of my tattered sari, when I longed to give my children fresh milk from the udders of our family cow which we had left behind.

Every evening, waiting for my husband to bring some money to buy food, I felt the colours which had eluded me the whole day come back to me with my tears as I sat watching the dry river bed. I imagined that there was water in the river just as in the full lake of our village. Sometimes, when I washed clothes in the little pool of water on the river bed where there was more sand than water, I sensed colour around me; the hand-dyed saris and bedsheets laid out to dry there would transform the little pool into a river of many colours. I would then forget my harsh world, and my heart would fly over the Sabarmati like a kingfisher.

To find some relief from the daily grind of my life I joined an adult education class. Till I went there I did not know how to write my name. Now, for hours I laboured over alphabets which had earlier meant nothing to me. It was then that I started lifting my veil to have a better look at the blackboard. I must say it felt better to see things clearly, and after months of hard work I felt a yellow ray of bright light emanating from the blackboard. Till then, I had always associated black with blood.

At the class I made friends with other women who had to face problems like mine, but they made a little extra money by cooking or washing dishes at a wedding hall near our hutments. Sometimes they brought back leftover food and sold it to us at a cheap price. At the class I rarely spoke but listened with interest to the chatter of the women from behind my veil. Slowly, colours began to reappear in my life in shades of green, orange, aubergine, blue and lemon yellow—almost like the colours of the vegetables, dals, fruits and clothes which we could never buy. Sometimes, I felt blinded with the intensity of my unrealized desires.

One day at the class, I heard the women talking about a wedding, and that the bride was looking for someone to paint traditional designs of peacocks and parrots on the compound walls of her house. I wanted to tell them that when I lived in the village, I was well known for the forms I used to paint on our walls during festivals like Diwali, Ganesh Chaturthi, Bhai-Bij and Karva Chauth. Painting was the only art I had learnt from my mother by helping her prepare the colours when she painted the walls of our house.

Just as I was about to tell them that I could paint, I was struck by a deep fear. I was not sure how my husband would react if I went to work outside the house without taking his permission. While I was thinking, a

form emerged from the darkness of my veil. It was that
of my elder son, standing naked and staring at a pile of
rotten fruit. This image pained me so deeply that I heard
myself saying I would go with them to paint the walls.

That night I returned home later than my husband. I
shivered behind my veil as I saw that his face was red—
not with blood but anger. As he saw the bag of flour and
fresh vegetables in my hand, bought with my own
earnings, he fell on me and began to beat me with his one
good hand till I fainted. He called me a prostitute,
assuming that I had taken to immoral ways, and my new-
found colours swirled around me like a whirlpool. Only
a few hours before I had mixed the colours to paint
Radha-Krishna surrounded by birds and animals, now the
same colours were lashing me with pain. He stopped
beating me only when the other women rushed into our
house to save me, and told him that I had earned the
money by painting. This seemed to cool him down.

Later that night he made up with me by eating out
of the same plate, and rays of yellow light mixed with the
shimmering blue of the river in spate coloured my vision.
It was difficult for his male ego to accept the fact that I
could also earn something by what I knew. But that night
he realized that we could not possibly survive if he did
not take my help.

Slowly, the colours of happiness returned in waves of
pink and silver, blue and gold, green and brown. Now,
when I see red it does not remind me of blood, but of
fired bricks, with which we hope to eventually build our
new home.

That was the beginning, since then I have received
many orders to paint walls for weddings and festivals.
Meanwhile, I love to paint the scenes of my village, the

big tree by the lake, the cows in the fields, the village well, the swing, the courtyard, the temple, the peacocks and the parrots, and of course my beautiful blue Krishna. As a painter, I do not suffocate in my veil any more. I lift my veil and look at the colours of life . . .

The Boyfriend

Our mother, Sabarmati, took away our hut last year. It had never rained as it rained that night. The river took away everything we had. We were left only with the clothes we were wearing. The sirens and the radio had warned us, but we had trusted Sabarmati.

With plastic bags on our heads we waited for the rain to stop. The tin roof of a shop by the road could not protect us for long. When the rain lessened we walked back to our house, only to find that we had neither a home nor any land to rebuild it on. My mother accepted our fate with folded hands and tears streaming down her face. I felt an anger rising in me for both mothers.

The landlord refused to rent out any land to us unless we gave him money or jewellery. We had nothing. Father earned only enough for us to eat once a day. All we had been able to salvage was an aluminium pot floating in the river and a goat which adopted us. A black piece of plastic was our roof. We huddled close to each other with the goat to keep us warm and I was suddenly dreaming of the drought which had driven us out of our village. I was fourteen then, and the sun had dried my cheeks like the earth. The rain had been a beautiful desire. In the stark white sky I would paint a blue cloud with my thoughts and smell the fresh coolness of the rain falling softly on my cheeks. And now I was sitting in the rain, huddled with my three younger brothers and two little sisters. One died that night. She was two months old.

Father found an old rag to wrap her and we walked to the crematorium in the rain. Again we found ourselves on the river bed and I felt as if my father was offering my sister as a sacrifice to the river. Babies are not cremated, so she was buried. The crematorium gave some relief. We sat under the huge roof where our clothes dried with the warmth from the dying embers of another cremation.

The rain stopped after three days. Mother bought some flour from the grocer on credit and made chapattis on a wood fire. Father went back to loading trucks.

What he earned was not enough to feed all of us, so I worked as a maidservant in the apartments across the road. I cleaned and cooked in five houses. The money, food and old clothes from these houses kept us alive. The goat had also grown and we had milk for breakfast. But Father was restless. We needed a home with brick walls, a tin roof and perhaps a proper bathroom. Now, Mother held a cloth around me while I bathed, and I did the same for her. We also had to walk quite a distance to reach the toilets, while my brothers and younger sister squatted on the pavement itself. For the home of our dreams, we needed money.

Then, one day, a schoolteacher I worked for asked me if I would like to work in a school. I was seventeen years old then and was soon earning two hundred rupees for sweeping the classrooms and filling water. Every month we counted the money and with sinking hearts we knew that we would have to work for another three years to buy a pucca hut of our own; a place that would only belong to us, where there would be no fear of the police, the municipal encroachment vans, the rain, the sun and the dogs.

I met Mohun at the school. He worked there as a peon in the principal's office. He lived in the slums by the river with his old mother and was deep in debt with the moneylender after he had had to borrow money in order to pay for his sister's dowry. He was small and thin, but very kind to me and often we shared a saucer of bitter-sweet tea from the corner shop.

He took me to see my first Hindi film. I felt like a thief, but slowly I learnt to enjoy the false world of songs and tears. By our third film, I allowed Mohun to touch my breast. Going to the cinema offered a great relief from the reality of my existence. It became our escape. But my dual life was making me desperate. I wanted to be free of my parents and run away with Mohun, just like in the films we saw. My dream house was also like something in a film. A small apartment with brightly coloured walls and delicate pink curtains; a sparkling white-tiled bathroom, a cooking range with stainless steel dishes and a blue formica-topped table. A red scooter for us to go to the cinema, and gold necklaces hidden in a cupboard full of polyester saris—one for each song.

I was surprised to see an apartment almost like my dreams when I was offered work as a full-time maidservant in a rich family. They lived in London and their father lived alone here. He had fractured his leg and I was supposed to look after him. I had very good references and looked trustworthy. In a day, my life changed. I earned five hundred rupees a month for cooking, cleaning, and washing clothes. This also included feeding and washing the old man.

I had a room to myself, and for the first time in my life, I slept on a real bed with my head on a pillow, instead of huddling on the pavement with the goat. Though I must admit that I was afraid of being locked into the bathroom and I could not sleep the first few nights without the warmth of bodies around me. For a long time I lay awake thinking about my family.

What started like a dream did not last long, because soon Mohun taught me to cheat. When all was quiet at night he came to meet me by telling the watchman that he was my brother. I left the front door open, and unknown to my employer, Mohun slept with me.

The old man never recovered from his fall and spent his time reading newspapers and playing chess with friends. He slept and ate at regular times, and allowed me to watch the television. The family had also given me a radio, which I kept in the kitchen. Sometimes, the old man scared me by watching me silently and I wondered whether he knew about Mohun, although I had won his confidence and he had even given me the keys of his cupboard.

But then life, like films, is full of difficulties. One day, as I sponged the old man and helped him into his pyjamas, I felt the pressure of his hands on my breasts.

He was pulling me towards him and I allowed him. Tears were running down his withered cheeks and I could see both loneliness and lust in his eyes.

This became a habit. Each time he would slip me some money. My mind went blank every time he touched me. I learnt to detach myself from what was happening. On such days I switched on the television and drowned myself in the sound. We never spoke. It was like watching a film with the sound switched off.

That year Father bought land in the slums and started building a house with the help of my brothers. He also planned to get me married that year. But that was not the end of our troubles. Mohun refused to marry me. He said he was in debt, and he could marry me only if I helped him financially. I felt like the bird which everyone coveted only because of the golden eggs it laid. There had been a certain freedom in our needs and hungers. I was lost. Mohun's greed along with my family's needs were worse than the old man's lust. I made the mistake of a lifetime when I told Mohun about the money in the house. From that day on he was after me to help him steal it. I spent the days in a daze, as I did not like the idea of losing faith with the family in London. Then one night, he came to the house and strangled the old man, but could not find the money as I refused to tell him where it was. The coward ran away.

The next morning, as I sat on a rickety chair at the police station, gazing at the dry Sabarmati from the window, I fell into a doze and dreamt that it was the night after the floods. Far away I could hear the dogs barking and I was looking for the corpse of my sister. I was digging the river's womb with my nails. When I found her—I was looking at my own face.

Mother

Every morning when my parents go to unload the trucks of grain on the other end of Ellis Bridge, Mother feeds my brother and leaves some goat milk, which I feed him through the day. In the evenings, when they return, Mother always walks ahead of Father and starts running when she reaches our pavement. Her breasts become painful with the milk, as it soaks her sari through the blouse. When my brother takes her breast, tears of relief fill her eyes.

I have been looking after my younger brothers and sisters since I was five years old. I can proudly say that I have brought up all my brothers and sisters, because what with Mother's pregnancies and the many mouths to feed, both Mother and Father have had to work hard, so that we have something to eat at the end of the day.

While they are away, we play on the pavement which is our home. We do not go to school, so we entertain ourselves by teasing the schoolchildren passing by in their clean uniforms. In this way, we forget hunger and our desire for new clothes and toys. I once found a huge tattered doll in a garbage bin which must have looked like me, because she had hair like a crow's nest and a torn dress like the one I have been wearing for the past three years.

Every year, before the festivals, Mother promises to buy new clothes for us. But then, every year there is a pregnancy to take care of, and a new baby. Besides that, Father has been trying to save money so that we can buy a shack on the bank of the river, where there are many huts under the Gandhi bridge. I look at my torn dress and think perhaps next year I will get a new one. I do not know what I look like. None of us know what we look like.

Once we tried to look at ourselves in the glass of the new shopping centre being built nearby. I was standing in front of the huge glass windows with my little brother on my hip and suddenly realized that I was looking at myself. At first I thought that the ragged doll from the garbage bin had come alive and was watching me. My mother tells me I am twelve years old and have big black eyes. So I went closer to the glass to see how big my eyes were. But as my nose touched the glass, I was suddenly flung on the pavement by the watchman.

A minute later I was running and crying at the same time, as the man had threatened to break my brother's head with his baton. He was shouting at me and calling me a thief. They always call us thieves. When I had looked at my reflection in the window I had not realized that there was food and clothing behind the big glass walls. Things I knew I can never have. How was I to explain to the watchman that the moment of looking at my reflection had been one of innocence.

But let me tell you what happened to my brother. He was crying for Mother since morning, although she had fed him before leaving for work. She must have heard him crying, but she could not run back and hold him in her arms; she was already late for work and could not afford to lose the money.

At first I thought he was hungry. Then I assumed that he had a stomach ache because he was teething. He refused to drink the goat milk which I tried to force down his throat. He choked on it and threw up all over me. He was crying so much that I could not even clean myself.

I walked him. I sang to him. I talked to him. But he would not stop crying, and I was tired of carrying him and wanted to throw him on the pavement. I just wanted to rest on my quilt for a while and run on the streets like a bird, without the burden of any of my brothers or sisters.

At the end of the day my brother was crying so much that pedestrians were telling me to take care of him. I was so angry with him that I threatened to throw him under the bus. But it was of no use. He seemed to be crying much more than before, so I also sat down on the ground and cried with him.

I was frightened, as he seemed to get the hiccups and looked as though he was fainting. I thought I had killed my brother.

I wanted my mother, but did not know where she was. Then I did what my mother would have done to stop him from crying. I opened my blouse and gave him the nipple of my yet unformed breast. He stopped crying and looked up at me. He did not know the difference, and I was crying like my mother.

Ghosts

My own children run away from me. My youngest never comes near me. For all her needs she goes to my elder sister-in-law who looks after my children and is very good to them. She oils their hair and removes the lice.

To remove lice is boring. It takes hours, as one has to oil the hair and inspect it, and having located the louse, catch it between the forefinger and thumb. The louse must not fall. It has to be carefully transferred onto the nail and squashed. This calls for a very delicate coordination of the eyes and fingers. The dead lice are then collected on a dirty rag, counted and thrown away.

When there are hundreds of lice in the hair, it can be

very tiring. So, whenever my mother comes to see me, she first checks my hair. She even tries to frighten me by telling me that ghosts are attracted to lice. But this story does not scare me.

There is a reason why my sister-in-law spends hours on my children's hair. Once when there were too many lice in my youngest daughter's hair, I pulled at it so hard that she screamed and my sister-in-law rushed out to see what was happening. I had then casually mentioned that the sight of lice made me feel like burning my daughter's hair. Since then I have been free of her hair.

When they see me watching her hair, I see fear in everybody's eyes. In fact they fear me for more things than I am aware of. If I laugh too much, for no definite reason, I see fear. If I am sad, if I do not talk or answer questions regarding my health, they look at me suspiciously. Often I am happy to say nothing. I do not understand what they expect me to say. Either I talk too much or laugh too much or not at all. If I sit and stare at nothing, they worry for me. If I keep on feeling the cavity in my molar, it's again no good. If I feel like dancing or singing in the middle of the road it is not correct. Because, they say, a grown-up woman does not behave like that. On some days I wake up feeling so low that I do not wash or cook. So my sister-in-law, my husband's elder brother's wife, takes care of both houses.

She works as a farmhand in a suburb of Ahmedabad. While I sit at home and suffocate, every evening my sister-in-law returns looking fresh and beautiful from the open spaces, holding a bouquet of radishes. This sight makes me sick. Her husband is a peon in an office and mine works as a servant in a cloth store. They do not earn enough and she works hard so that there is always a little extra for the children's school dresses and lunch boxes.

Everybody says she is a good woman. So I dislike her. I never let her know. Because then she would not do all that she does for me. But I have a suspicion that she knows. Unlike her, I prefer to sit and brood under the tamarind tree.

They say the tree is the cause of all my problems. But I like to sleep under it and listen to the rustle of leaves.

A distant aunt from our village had suggested that they get me treated by a witch doctor. He came on a dark moonless night. In the dim light of the kerosene lantern I could not see his face very well. He was as dark as the night and was wearing a green vest which had parrots embroidered on it. He was holding a broom of peacock feathers in his hand.

The family sat outside the door. I cringed in a corner as he lit a small fire in a clay stove. Then he stood up and adjusted his loincloth. He was skinny, but he had a large head with long hair, and was wearing coloured glass beads around his neck which made him look fierce. Without all these trappings he would look like a boy. My own husband is built very much like that. Then he opened a cloth bag and took out a drum made of goat intestines and played a beat on it with a small wooden stick. When he hit me with the peacock-feather broom, I screamed. The man saw my tearful anger. At this he was very pleased and asked the ghost to leave me. He was talking to it and saying, 'You entered her on a moonless night when she was sleeping under the tamarind tree. It was just after midnight, the time when you like to roost on trees with your legs turned backwards. You looked down and saw this poor woman, and unfortunately on that particular day she had broken a pimple on her left temple, and so there was a hole in her forehead. You entered from there and made a seat for yourself.

'Then, the other evening she passed a well, where another spirit saw the hair full of lice and was attracted to them. It lives in her ears and so this poor woman cannot hear any more.

'The third spirit entered her when she was walking past a dry tree in the afternoon. An unlikely time, but her mouth was open and she was laughing. It entered her from a cavity in her tooth and since then she cannot eat like before.

'The fourth spirit found a way from the navel when she was cleaning it while having a bath in the open. This is the most troublesome for the family, as she does not feel hungry, and does not cook for them any more. This poor woman is suffering just because of the passage you made in her forehead.'

As he said this he threw a handful of dry red chillies in the fire. The smoke from the chillies was unbearable. My eyes burnt from it and I felt suffocated. I thought there were spirits dancing around me, trying to kill me. I was naturally frightened. I tried to run, but the witch doctor was beating me with the peacock feathers and I was screaming.

Then I fainted. The next day I woke up feeling depressed. I was thinking about myself. I have been unhappy from the day I married. I do not like my husband. I had hoped to marry his elder brother. He is manly and caring. He is married to my sister, who happens to be my sister-in-law.

The First Wife

She was the queen of the city's largest slum under the busy Nehru Bridge where the river is but a trickle. Here sand for the construction sites is collected on donkeys while dhobis wash clothes in the murky water and dyers dry their colourful saris on the dry river bed.

On the road outside the slum is a bazaar where vendors sell rotten vegetables, bitter-sweet tea, soda and leftover food from the wedding halls nearby. Most of the people living in the slum have a small business of buying and selling old gunny bags, newspapers and scrap.

The Queen's scrap-metal shop was situated at the entrance of the slum and she sat there on a wrought iron chair with a design of creepers. Her many children cleaned and sold the scrap as she supervised and counted the money, all the time loudly cursing her useless husband who sat at home drinking local liquor. She declared that she wished him dead, yet she returned home every afternoon to cook his lunch. While she lit the clay stove and ground the spices, she shared with her husband a bidi and a saucer of tea. The same ritual followed in the evening with fish or goat meat and a bottle of liquor.

I visited her shop often to look for some interesting pieces of scrap to fashion into pieces of sculpture. Often, when I bought a sizeable amount of scrap from her, she offered me a cold soda. She would be even more pleased if I sat in the shop for some time and shared a saucer of tea with her.

I had noticed her shop while passing by in an autorickshaw and had first entered it on a whim. Before that I had never entered a slum. She took me inside the slum and showed me a new world. The large sprawling place amazed me and I wondered how people lived in such crowded surroundings. While we walked, a child was always at her breast and the younger children followed us around. The older ones were either playing or gambling or sleeping on the cars to be sold as scrap kept outside her shop. None of them went to school except one son who was a teacher. He lived in a separate house with his wife.

Laxmi had become the uncrowned queen of the slum during the communal riots. She had stood at the entrance of the slum at midnight, large and frightening in the seventh month of her pregnancy with a sword in her hand, like a goddess guarding the slum. She was fearless.

She became the undisputed leader after the police

took her away and charged her for keeping a sword and a country-made revolver. She was soon released and came out victorious from the police lock-up. The slum people held her in great esteem after that, especially when the police began to stop often at her shop and have tea with her.

Many a night she slept outside her shop and guarded the scrap from thieves. People said that she only had to cough and they would run away. Even the mounted police who went past her shop on their horses asked her if she needed help. She was treated like an elder and everybody took her advice for personal problems. Yet she never asked anybody for help, though I could see that her frequent pregnancies were wearing her down. Her husband, a thin, shrivelled alcoholic, sat in the shack the whole day cursing her and ridiculing her status in the slum.

It was only when she was heavy and tired with her eleventh child that she asked me to help her. She had heard an announcement on the radio but was too shy to ask anybody about it. But she had decided that she did not want any more children as it was difficult to bring them up. She was exhausted, yet afraid that an operation would kill her. When I explained to her that it was a simple procedure, she agreed to go through with a tubectomy.

Before she got admitted to the municipal hospital, she made arrangements for her house and shop as all her elder daughters were married and the younger children did not understand the seriousness of her problem. She asked a distant cousin to help her with the house while she was away for two weeks. The cousin was a young woman who had been recently divorced. I went to see Laxmi every day at the hospital and after two weeks brought her back to her house with her baby girl.

Later, busy with my own work and assuming all was well with the Queen, I did not go back to see her for two months. When I did, I was alarmed as she was not sitting on her throne at the entrance of the shop. Instead, a rather rude old man, whom I assumed to be her husband, was sitting there. He told me that Laxmi did not live there any more and that he did not know her whereabouts.

After three years, I met her again in the most unusual circumstances. One day, as I was looking for an address in a housing society, suddenly a beggar woman with a child ran towards me and held on to me. For a moment I was frightened as I thought she was mad. She was not, it was the Queen, embracing me with tears running down her dirty cheeks.

My shoulder was wet with her tears and a small crowd had collected around us. Someone asked me if I needed help. Too moved for words, I stopped an autorickshaw and brought her to my house.

She refused to enter my drawing room saying she was too dirty, so we sat in the garden, where she washed herself and fed her daughter with biscuits and tea. She had shrunk and her skin was no longer like copper. Her lips trembled when she spoke and tears filled her eyes as she told me her story.

The cousin who had come to look after her house while she was in hospital had decided to make Laxmi's house her own. She found a willing partner in Laxmi's husband.

When Laxmi returned, she immediately realized that things had changed. She was angry, but her husband, instead of showing penitence, called her a whore in the hearing of the crowd that had collected, dragging her by the hair in front of the people who had once respected her like a goddess.

She was totally humiliated. More was to follow. Her husband called the local witch doctor to decide if she had been unfaithful to him. Amidst the sound of drums and the sacrifice of a black goat, the seeds thrown by the witch doctor fell in a design which did not favour Laxmi and she was proved to be immoral. Her husband then alleged that the last child was not his, and perhaps belonged to some policeman. These allegations infuriated Laxmi and she called upon a committee of elders to decide her fate. But they, too, believed the witch doctor's verdict, unaware that he had been bribed by Laxmi's husband.

Laxmi finally lost her battle when she realized that she had failed to check upon the fact that the house and shop were registered as her husband's property. She lost her little scrap-metal business to him. To add to this, the children did not want to become homeless with her and stayed on in the house with their father. They knew the law of the jungle that existed on the pavements for the homeless. Quietly, with tears in their eyes, they watched her go.

The people who had once held her in esteem did not stop her. They suspected her of infidelity. They could not respect an unfaithful woman. Nobody gave Laxmi a chance to explain, nor did they offer her shelter. The only educated son of the family refused to help, as he was ashamed of her.

Laxmi was suddenly left with no one but her infant daughter. She had to start all over again, with the pavement as her home. Sitting there, she was thinking about her life, when someone threw some coins at her feet and she realized that she had become a beggar. She was no longer the queen.

Maya Desai

I had inherited my mother's unusual beauty, her perfect features and almond eyes which always seemed half closed and slanted upwards—like the sculptures of the vidyadharis at the temple. Sometimes, when Mother looked into the mirror to make a bindi with kumkum, she seemed to sigh. Years later, I had understood it to be a sigh of deep disappointment, because Father never seemed to notice how beautiful she was. For him she was the childbearer, the mother of his precious son and three daughters. She was the caretaker of the house. But I had seen my own face staring back at me from the sepia wedding photo in their room.

By the time I was thirteen, I was aware of my beauty by the looks I received in the street and from the boys in my class. Unlike my sisters Ketki and Mayuri, I was tall and well formed. This annoyed them, and sometimes they fought with me for no reason at all, scratching my face or pulling my hair till I screamed and hit them back. When Mother wanted to know about the red gashes on my face, my sisters kept quiet, their eyes on the floor, and I told her that I had scratched my face by mistake.

The constant stares of people as they looked at my copper-coloured skin, slanting kohl-filled eyes, full lips and slim, svelte figure made me decide that I needed to protect myself. I stopped smiling and looking people in the eye. I donned a mask. I played this game so well that even my sisters were no longer jealous of me. With a lot of practice, I acted as though I was just a beautiful face without warmth or intelligence. The distant look made people leave me alone as if I was a sculpture.

Secretly, I enjoyed appreciative looks, and the knowledge of my good looks was like being high on bhang. I was addicted to my own looks and to appear beautiful was more important than anything else. The constant effort I had to make at not looking human was painful, but my mask also made me feel secure. I did not want to go beyond that to face the person within me. It was an armour against hurt, and because I kept away from everybody and spoke only when I was spoken to, I saved myself from everything that could harm me. My mask was like my bodyguard.

Sometimes I would imagine myself without it and I would be terrified. Without it I felt naked and exposed, as though I had no skin. While walking on the street, or to the bus stand or any place where there were crowds, it was easier to move unseen and faceless. The mask became a part of my being.

Then one day, I felt love and desire stirring within me and I decided to remove my mask and face life. I had joined the municipal swimming pool, and he was my instructor. Under water, I was just a woman called Maya and he was a man named Jaladhi. The male and the female—there was nothing else between us. I felt we were the eternal couple—water nymphs—facing each other in the transparency of water.

Later, alone in his room, I allowed him to touch my eyes and kiss me. When we became one, I could no longer return home. In his warm and urgent embraces, I came into my own and did not need to wear a mask any more. We were married in a temple, and left for Bombay the same night to take the blessings of Jaladhi's parents. In the train, again I felt eyes hovering around me, as I knew I looked very beautiful in a red bandhni sari. I was about to slip on my mask, but I looked into Jaladhi's eyes and felt safe. I could now live without the mask.

Jaladhi's mother was not happy with our secret marriage. She made me feel as if I had snared her innocent son. I felt the mask creeping up and spreading all over my face. That night Jaladhi stared into my eyes and said, 'Tonight, somehow I do not recognize you.' I decided to remain silent, and we spent four uncomfortable days with his parents.

Back in Ahmedabad, my parents had started searching for me. The disappearance of a daughter was a matter of great discussion in the community. Mother was sure that someone had kidnapped me. But Father did not want to register a police case as his friend, Hirakaka, had told him that he had seen me with Jaladhi in a restaurant. He asked all my friends about my whereabouts but nobody knew where we were. Instead they told my parents that I was secretive and never told them anything about myself.

My father found Jaladhi's Bombay address from the municipal swimming pool office, and one morning I opened the door to find him standing there. I felt a great sense of relief, and with my tears my mask melted into nothingness. When the elders had accepted the situation, they decided to have a celebration—both in Bombay and Ahmedabad. Jaladhi and I were happy that night, and as we embraced, he said, 'Tonight you look more like the Maya I know.'

For the hurriedly held wedding reception, my mother arrived with my sisters and brother, Sumant. That evening, when she was helping me with the sky-blue zari sari which my mother-in-law had given me, she whispered with tears in her eyes, 'Could you not have waited till I had married off Mayuri and Ketaki? They are older than you, how will I find grooms for them now that you have done this? Don't you know what an elopement means in our community? And with our limited finances, nobody will marry them.'

The evening turned sour for me. Once again I slipped on my mask. Jaladhi's relatives and friends congratulated him for having abducted an apsara for a wife. But my smile was frozen, my eyes were still, and I felt neither warmth nor pleasure. It was the same when we had another party in Ahmedabad. I felt like a convict who is to be hanged the next morning. But for the world I had a fixed smile on my face.

Back in our rented one-room house, life was not the romantic vision of my dreams. It was a struggle. I still had to finish college and we could not manage on what

Jaladhi earned. So, in a week, my life became a whirlwind of work and worries.

I got up early, cooked lunch, and left for college. After that I worked as a receptionist in a travel agency. In the evening I would be very tired, but all I could afford was the city bus. Once I reached my house, I had no energy to cook the evening meal. But I had to.

Slowly, as our passion started to wear off, I resented that Jaladhi lazed at home all day long, unshaven and slovenly. It never occured to him that since he had to be at the swimming pool only in the mornings and late evenings, he could look for a part-time job and help me run the household.

When I finished college, I had to immediately look for work, although I wanted to study further. When I was selected as an accountant in a bank, Jaladhi was happy. It had never occured to him to ask me whether I wanted to study or work. He assumed that it was the most natural thing on earth that I should work. Leading our separate lives, gradually we became isolated from each other. If he did not recognize me as the same Maya, I did not know who he was either. Drained of all emotion, we were like two harsh, cruel animals.

Yet, within I still yearned for music, for flowers. Instead, silent like a mannequin, I walked, worked, and when we made love, he never asked me, 'Tonight why do you look different?'

He was so used to my mask by now that he could not make out the difference between the real and the unreal. And under its skin, I could feel the river within me dying. I could no longer look at Jaladhi without searching for the other Jaladhi floating on a deep blue surface with me hovering over him like a bright dragonfly.

One day we went for lunch to Jaladhi's friend, Sushil's house who worked in Dubai. For years Sushil had worked as a peon in the telephone department and had a tough time making ends meet. Then he found work in Dubai. He had returned home after three years, and the change we saw in their little house took our breath away. There was the smell of fresh paint, a new sofa set and a brand new formica dining table. On the shelves stood a CD player and a television set. His wife Malti had every possible gadget in the kitchen. She was wearing an expensive sari and it was impossible not to notice her diamond ring. All through lunch, as she gushed about her husband and their latest acquisitions, I could not help notice Jaladhi's silence, and the faraway look in his eyes.

When we took the bus home, he told me in a tone that brooked no argument that he intended to leave for Dubai and make his fortune. I guessed he had been struck by Malti's praise for her husband and had decided to prove to me that eventually he would earn more than me. He would not live on my earnings. I wondered, if Jaladhi returned from Dubai with a fat bank balance and a bag of diamonds, would I gush about him the way Malti did? I had my doubts.

We knew it was finally over as I waved goodbye to him when he left. On my own, it was not easy. I could still feel Jaladhi's presence in the house and I decided to erase it. Suddenly I felt like the musk deer who does not know the source of the heady fragrance that comes from the nether regions of its body. With Jaladhi's departure, I first encouraged Saurabh. But my affairs did not seem to last. I ended up with three lovers in a row—Saurabh, Kirit and Amol. They all thought I was strange. Then one day Mother came to see me. As a silent protest, she had never come to my house. I had always visited her. She had arranged for the weddings of Ketaki and Mayuri with great difficulty and always thought that she could have done better if it had not been for me.

Mother had come to take me back home. She did not tell me, but from her eyes I could see that she had heard about what she would call my bad ways. And I was tired. I needed the shelter and comfort of being with Mother. I had left her when I was not prepared for the difficulties of life.

When I went to live with Mother, I received an offer to act in a television serial. Saurabh had spoken to someone about my looks and possible acting abilities. For a moment, I felt as if the river within was in full spate. Yes, I had always wanted to act. Had I been alone, I would have consented without a thought. But I knew that Mother's first reaction would be a refusal. And it was. She did not want me to cross the threshold of our house again. But now I was a grown-up woman and I convinced her that she allow me to at least give a screen test. My brother helped by arguing with her that something artistic would keep me busy. The matter left a heavy silence between Mother and me.

The successful screen test proved to me that I was a born actress. In front of the camera, I unmasked myself and released the floodgates of all my pent-up emotions. In some time I became a much sought after actress for both theatre and television. I could move the audience to tears with my acting. But once I removed my make-up, the mask slipped back into its place effortlessly. This double life suited me very well, and I learnt to ignore Mother's complaints about late nights. In fact, for the first time in my life, I was happy.

For two years I reigned over the television and theater world. Then Jaladhi returned, but only for two months and I was back to my old world. Mother insisted that I go back to my own house. Picking up the threads of our old life, we lived as before. This was not difficult now as I could rip away my mask the moment I put on my make-up for the stage. I had expected Jaladhi to put an end to my acting career. He did not; instead, surprisingly, he encouraged me. My fame suited him.

Then he went back and I had two more years to myself. In this four-year period, Maya Desai became a name to be reckoned with. No doubt there were moments when I suddenly woke up with a start in the middle of the night and asked myself, who am I? I could go back to sleep only after I had reassured myself that I was Maya Desai, the actress!

At the end of his four-year stay in Dubai, Jaladhi returned for his usual holiday. I assumed he would go back after a couple of months, but he did not. With a shock I realized that he was back for good. When he confirmed my doubts, I was shattered. Worse was to follow. He stopped encouraging me to work, and we had big fights over my late nights. He alleged that I was an unfaithful wife. This affected my work and slowly, my directors started telling me to put more life into my roles. I started feeling tired and spent.

Finally, Jaladhi played his last card. One night, I came back late, having worked for three shifts to find him waiting for me with food he had bought from a restaurant. I was naturally pleased, and that night we made love after a long time. Then he surprised me with a shower of gifts. He covered my naked body with diamonds and gold bangles, placing one huge diamond on my forehead. I felt as though I was the night sky and the full moon was shining between my eyebrows. Then suddenly I felt terrified—was I wearing a mask of jewels? Or was I glowing like a thousand candles that people light for the dead in some faraway land? I could not stand up, I could not look at myself in the mirror.

The next morning, I realized that this had been Jaladhi's way of telling me that he was now a rich man and I need not go out of the house. He had plans to start a business of fibre glass chairs, and he commanded that once I had finished my assignments, I should stay at home and start a family. He had also taken my mother in his confidence and she wanted a promise from me that I would not accept any more acting assignments. She felt I had given the family enough of a bad name and ruined my life.

I was taken aback by the turn of events and could not find Maya Desai, try as I might. I felt helpless. My mask had fallen, and I could not find it. Suddenly, my face had become a sparkling mirror of jewels; a flat shining surface for others to admire and in which Jaladhi could see his own reflection. Without Maya Desai the actress between us, our occasional embraces seemed to hurt me, as though glass was being crushed in the circle of our arms. Faces and masks—both frightened me.

Jaladhi tormented me. Having placed me on a pedestal like a bejewelled goddess, he had broken my mask and cut it into tiny pieces. Wounded, I stood exposed and bleeding. Yet, I could hear a river flowing within me. Was it an earth spring or a volcano? No, it was my own blood—warm, pulsating and rebelling against Jaladhi's violence.

I was Jaladhi's prisoner. He tortured me, he beat me,

he slapped me—and with extreme violence he put an end
to my acting career. As for me, without Maya Desai I did
not know how to live. Our new bungalow suffocated me,
and though I tried, I could not find my mask—my
protector. In Jaladhi's jewelled mirror, I could not see my
face. All I felt was the great burden of Jaladhi standing
on my shoulders. I could not escape the fence he had
built around me.

Besides that, Mother wanted me to stay in my
husband's house, and I had no strength to jump out and
swim away to make my own life. Perhaps I could—I had
enough money and some friends. All I had to do was find
myself a flat and fight Jaladhi. So easy to say, but not easy
to do. I felt helpless, trapped, afraid and alone. Caught
between Jaladhi and Mother, I had no voice, no escape,
except one . . . I locked myself in the privacy of the blue
tiled bathroom with its imported faucets. The smell of
kerosene was spreading all over me—while the bottles of
French perfumes stood unopened on the rack. And then,
all I could see were bright orange flames. The tongues of
death were encircling me. Fire. I would burn the maskless
Maya on the sandalwood pyre of her desires. And then,
Maya Desai would no longer search for Maya Desai . . .

Amina

This story was narrated to me by Langha Ahmedbhai Savabhai of village Dasada, now living in the Gupta Nagar slums of Ahmedabad, during the one-month death ceremony of Langha Kalubhai Mohmedbhai.

*

Our body is in the limits of the head and the toes of our feet. The hand, the shoulder, the knee, the thigh and the waist lead us to the stomach, which is so deep that a man spends a whole lifetime filling it. After this, there is the chest and the neck which holds the head and the brain— the most precious and valuable part of our body.

Above all this we wear garments which conceal our body. When there is a stain on our clothes, we try to remove it with water. If it does not go, we use soap and soda, or else we give our clothes to a dhobi. If nothing helps we discard the garment. Likewise, a stain on one's life distresses a person more than anything else. This is a story about the many incidents of my life which could have been like stains, but I did not allow them to leave their marks on me.

My earliest memories are of my cousin Fatma, the daughter of my uncle Malabhai Jugajibhai. She was older than me, but we used to play together. When we received an invitation from Malabhai for her engagement ceremony, I could not go, as there was some misunderstanding between my father and Uncle. This incident made me feel very helpless as Fatma would have been happy to see me there.

My father's name was Galabhai Jugajibhai and Nathi was my mother's name. Her brother Adambhai lived with us as they had lost their parents when they were young, and my father had to look after both Adambhai and his fields.

In our family Adambhai was looked after like a prince. I remember, sometimes at night he would throw tantrums and refuse to sleep on his own bed. Instead, he would insist on sleeping on my father's shoulder, who would spend many a sleepless night sitting with Adambhai in his lap. He fulfilled all of Adambhai's wishes, whims and fancies.

In those days, it was considered to be prestigious to become a driver. The Dasada royal family owned four cars, and Rasulbhai, our neighbour, worked as a driver there. When Adambhai decided to become a driver, my father took him to meet Rasulbhai, who agreed to teach Adambhai the basics of driving. In those days, one learnt driving by becoming an apprentice and living in the teacher's house. So Adambhai went to live with Rasulbhai. After that, although my father was certain that Rasulbhai took good care of Adambhai, he would often watch him from our window which opened into Rasulbhai's courtyard.

The day Adambhai received his driving licence, Father celebrated with a dinner party for our community, although we could not afford it. Father never disclosed our financial problems to Adambhai. Soon after, he celebrated Adambhai's engagement to Julekhabi. It was then that another misunderstanding took place between Father and Uncle Malabhai. Uncle informed my father that he would not attend Adambhai's engagement as his daughter Hava had not been invited. Hava was then married and living in Baroda.

When this news reached my father he was greatly distressed. The only person who could pacify him was the groom himself, who was busy dressing up for the engagement. The women were tying strings of flowers on his wrists and everyone was laughing. There was nobody available to go to Baroda and pacify Malabhai except Mankhan, a friend of Adambhai's, who had built the only double storey house in Dasada in those days, besides the royal palace. That is why I remember him.

That night, half asleep, I was watching Adambhai looking very grand with a sword, flowers and a string of gold beads around his neck. He was discussing with Mankhan the problem that Malabhai had created, and as I dozed off, I heard him asking Mankhan whether it was possible to go to Baroda and return the same night. All the while, I noticed they were casting worried glances at the door, as it was raining heavily.

I do not know when Adambhai and Mankhan left for Baroda. When everybody woke up the next morning, the women started crying, saying the bridegroom had disappeared. But by afternoon the tears turned into laughter when the bridegroom and Mankhan returned from Baroda with Malabhai and Havabibi's family. We left for Mandal, where the wedding was to take place, and stayed there for three days, revelling in the festivities, returning to Dasada on the fourth day. We were all very happy.

After Adambhai married Julekhabi, they shifted to Vanod where he worked as a driver. They were happily married for five years. Then, suddenly, Julekhabi fell ill and died. My father could not bear to see Adambhai lonely, so I went to stay with him, as Father was still looking after Adambhai's fields and other properties. He travelled between Vanod and Dasada with my mother, while I stayed on with Adambhai. I was still in my teens, but I cooked for both of us. Besides that, since a very young age I was keen on working, so Adambhai bought me a small stall where I would sell paan and bidis. Soon the business became profitable and Adambhai was very pleased with me. We were living quite comfortably but Adambhai was lonely and so my father started discussing with him the possibility of his marrying Rajobai, the daughter of Nathubhai Meghabhai of Bajana. Soon after broaching the subject with Nathubhai, my father died and we were faced with unexpected financial difficulties. Yet, Nathubhai agreed to give his daughter in marriage to Adambhai as it was a promise he had given my father.

After his marriage, Adambhai shifted to Patdi and

became a driver for Dadumaster's passenger buses which ran between Vanod and Viramgam. Later he left this job to drive Ambalalbhai's trucks. Often, when I went to Patdi to meet him, he would take me for a drive in his truck, but refused to teach me driving as I did not have the money to pay him for the lessons. I returned to Dasada disheartened and hurt, because Adambhai had forgotten all that my father had done for him.

Yet, whenever Adambhai was driving past Dasada to meet my mother, I would pester him to find me work as a helper on one of Ambalalbhai's trucks. Helpers on trucks have to work hard. They have to load, unload, fill cans of petrol, pump air in the tyres. So Adambhai would brush me off by saying that I could not work so hard. But I would insist, 'Find me a job and see how I work.' He finally found me work as a helper and I went to live with him. As a helper I also learnt how to drive.

In the meantime I was married to Amina. Suddenly, one day, Adambhai asked me to look for a separate house, because of Amina. While living with Adambhai what had hurt me most was that Aunt Rajobai had instigated Adambhai against Amina, who was not very beautiful. He would scold her, find faults with her and ask me to throw her out of the house, so that he could bring a better wife for me. But I had no complaint against Amina. We loved each other. But to please Adambhai, I sent her away to her father's house.

Around that time, there was a wedding in the family. My uncle, Ukabhai, had sent an invitation to Adambhai but had not invited me or my mother. Yet Adambhai insisted that I get some new clothes made and go to the wedding. I refused, but he behaved as though he could not understand what I was saying. Spoilt by my father, he did not care about social norms. Besides that, he always listened to his wife's advice. He did not seem to bother about what I had to say in the matter and left for the wedding with Rajobai, who told me that she had made arrangements for my food with Bibankhala, the old widow who lived near by.

I did not answer. But as soon as they left, I packed my belongings and left their house. I rented a small room for myself. All on my own, I thought often about Amina, but did not know how to ask her to return.

Then it so happened that there was another wedding, this time in Uncle Malabhai's house. My cousin Fakir Ahmed was getting married. He called on me and said, 'Come to the wedding with your wife.'

I had not seen my wife for a year. But when I wrote to my father-in-law that I was going to Fakir Ahmed's wedding and that he should bring Amina to the Patdi bus stand on such and such date, he agreed. When I met them at the bus stand, he left Amina with me without a single word of reproach. We went to Dasada for the wedding and were happy with each other.

After a few months, I left my job at Patdi and returned with Amina to Dasada, where we stayed with my mother. We had some income from our fields, but that was not enough, so I took up a job as the village watchman. When Uncle Malabhai saw me on duty he immediately reprimanded me, saying that none of our ancestors had ever worked as watchmen, and that I was underestimating myself because I could easily find work as a driver. Then he told Harjivanbhai of Patdi that I was a good driver and that he should try me out. Leaving my wife with my mother, I started work as Harjivanbhai's driver. Later Amina joined me there, but we were still not on talking terms with Adambhai who also lived there. Yet, secretly I met Aunt Rajobai when Adambhai was not in town and told her how distressed I was because of my strained relationship with my uncle.

Soon Adambhai came to know about my visits to his house and left a message for me with Rajobai: 'If Ahmed comes again, tell him he cannot enter my house.' In an effort to mend matters, I sent word to him whenever I had a problem with my car. He always came, repaired the car, and if I offered him tea or cigarettes, he accepted them, but never spoke to me. But he never let anybody know that there was any misunderstanding between us. If by chance we were seated together in the village square, we shared tea and cigarettes as though everything was normal between us.

Suddenly one day, we received news of his death from his neighbour Dhanudosi. We all rushed to Adambhai's house. My mother wept bitterly over the fact that nobody had bothered to inform her about her own brother's death. Rajobai's relatives knew about the death but they did not come for the funeral, and although we had not been informed, ultimately it became our responsibility to bury Adambhai. For two months we performed all the ceremonies connected with his funeral, and yet one day when we went to Rajobai's house, there was a lock on her door. Dhanudosi told us that she had left for Viramgam to live with her brothers. I was deeply distressed that although I had taken the responsibility of my uncle's funeral, my aunt had not bothered to inform me about her departure.

After a few months Rajobai returned to Patdi to pack the rest of her belongings and leave for Viramgam. I met her and advised her to go to Vanod instead, where she still had Adambhai's fields. But she refused, saying that she had received the money from Adambhai's insurance and that would be enough for her.

She went back to her brothers' house and in a few years lost all that she had. To add to this, her brothers convinced her to remarry. The marriage soon ended in a divorce and again Rajobai was forced to return to her brothers' house. As the brothers were in dire need of money, they all decided to shift to Ahmedabad and look for work.

Soon, we regularly received news from relatives that Rajobai and her family lived a very difficult life in the slums of Gupta Nagar in Ahmedabad. My mother advised me that I should bring them to our house. But for a decision like this, I needed the consent of my wife Amina. She agreed to accept Rajobai's family and said that as she had no children of her own, she would accept Rajobai's children as her's. I had full faith in my wife, as she had always guarded the honour of our family.

When I went to Ahmedabad in my brother-in-law Hajibhai's taxi, Rajobai refused to leave Ahmedabad and told me harshly that she would rather become a beggar than go with me. Hajibhai tried to intervene, but it was useless. So my mother and I continued to look after my aunt's property in Vanod.

One day, when I was sitting at Rasulbhai's shop, he told me that Rajobai had celebrated the engagement of her daughter Zinnat to a boy of questionable character. I discussed this problem with my mother, who advised me that Rajobai should be convinced to break the engagement. I told her that it was impossible to speak to Rajobai.

Then Allah helped us. That year, I became a father and we were to celebrate the circumcision of my son

Mohammed Sharif. I took advantage of the occasion and went to give an invitation to my aunt's family. She tried to ward me off by saying that she would send her children to the ceremony after she had stitched new clothes for them. I did not trust her, so I told her that I would get new clothes stitched for them. By the grace of Allah, she sent her children with me.

Once again I became a regular visitor to my aunt's house, and eventually told her that she would have to break Zinnat's engagement. But she refused to accept her fault in the matter. Still I insisted and told her that she could tell Zinnat's in-laws that I, as her uncle, did not approve of the alliance and would take the entire responsibility for the break-up.

Rajobai was in a dilemma as our uncle Hasambhai and aunt Allarakhi were involved in the matter of the engagement and had made it a prestige issue. Allarakhi was then in Vanod, but when my aunt sent her the message about my opinion regarding Zinnat's engagement, she hired a taxi and rushed to Ahmedabad and spent the whole night convincing Rajobai that Zinnat's fiancé was a good boy. By morning, my aunt felt harassed by Allarakhi and called out to me. As soon as I entered the room, I saw that Hasambhai was sleeping in a corner and Allarakhi left the room in anger when she saw me.

With all the loud discussions, Hasambhai woke up and started talking about the engagement. Quietly I told him that our daughter Zinnat's life and prestige were in danger. Hasambhai understood what I was trying to say, and asked me to look for another groom for Zinnat, while he would take care of the requirements of breaking the engagement. Then he called Allarakhi and convinced her. Fortunately she understood and we made a truce by drinking tea together. My aunt and her family decided to return with us to Patdi, and with a light heart I started searching for a proper match for Zinnat.

After a few years, my mother died. We also lost our fields and those of my aunt's, because of a new law that said that those who tilled the land became the owners. We now faced poverty as what I earned was not enough, and destiny brought us back to the Gupta Nagar slums of Ahmedabad, when Hasambhai promised to give us a piece of land on which we could build a hut of our own.

With full faith in Hasambhai, we sold our houses in Dasada and Patdi and came to Ahmedabad. The day we left our house in Dasada, we cried, and we continue to cry till today, because we can never return to our home town.

Once we reached Ahmedabad, we discovered that we were homeless because Hasambhai, who had taken all our money, did not give us our land on the pretext that his partner had absconded with the cash. I was out on the streets, without money or proof, as it had never crossed my mind that I should have prepared some legal documents in connection with the land and the transfer of money. Besides, there was nobody who could intervene and help us out of our predicament. I broke down with the terrible burden of providing a roof for two families, mine and Rajobai's.

I looked around and found a piece of land at a little distance from the slums. Here Amina helped me tie a cloth over four poles, which would serve as a roof for us. Sensing the seriousness of the situation, even the children did not cry, nor did they ask for anything. Amina with her foresight had packed some flour in our baggage, and that night she made a stove of a few bricks and dry twigs and rolled out hot chapattis for our dinner. As we ate the dry chapattis, I thanked Allah that Amina was with me.

The next day, Amina did something she had never done before. She made friends with some women in the slums and found work for both of us as construction labourers. While we worked, Rajobai looked after the children and our belongings. But she was neither happy nor cooperative. Yet Amina took good care of her and did not give her any reason to complain. But it always distressed me that my aunt was never thankful—even to Allah.

Slowly we saved enough to buy a small hut in the heart of the Gupta Nagar slums. Our house was built over an unused, haunted step-well under a banyan tree. The land belonged to Jagabhai and his wife Kanta. Amina was not afraid of the haunted step-well, instead she was thankful to Allah that we had a roof over our head.

Amina worked very hard and was respected at the construction site for her sincere work. One day she asked the overseer for a loan, which she promised to pay back by working overtime. With the loan we repaired the roof and bought some pans and wheat. In those days, Amina was a pillar of strength, and although she was carrying our third child, she never complained. Quietly she had taken charge of everything.

In the village, I had never known Amina to have these qualities. When we lived in Patdi, she had never crossed the threshold of our house unless it was necessary. Perhaps I had never given her the scope to take decisions.

We worked very hard during the day, but at night we could barely catch up with our sleep as our neighbour Jagabhai's buffalo was tied near our house. She had a bad horn which she kept rubbing against our side of the wall.

Besides, there was a lot of slush around the animal, and this attracted insects and mosquitoes. All night we kept burning dry neem leaves to save the children from insect bites.

Rajobai did not want to live in a haunted house, so with our help she rented another small hut for her family. As she had never worked outside the house, we helped her out with food and clothing. To ease the situation, I also found work for her son as a waiter in a roadside dhaba near the octroi post.

In many ways the boy was like Adambhai, with a good head for business, and soon he bought a small tea stall of his own. But he did not have a kind heart. When our work at the construction site was over he made no move to help us, neither did my aunt say anything when we told her about our financial difficulties.

But Amina was undaunted. She discovered a small factory which made medicinal capsules. She made friends with the women who worked there and offered to work if and when one of them wanted to go on leave. Her only aim in life now was that none of the children should ever sleep on an empty stomach. At the time I was without work, and it distressed me. To ease my tension, I started cooking the evening meals for the family. When some men of our community saw me cooking, they called me a henpecked husband. This did not bother me and I continued to share with Amina the burden of work.

After I had been unemployed for two years, Hasambhai, who had cheated us, was moved by my plight and helped us by informing me that Dr Isapji, who lived near by, was looking for a driver. The day I drove the doctor to his clinic, I felt as light as a flower. But with four children, life was always difficult. Although Rajobai's family was doing very well, they never helped us. By then they had built a pucca house for themselves and were considered to be affluent in the slums. We were still their poor relatives. I was always alert about the problems of the slum, so with Jagabhai and others I made a group, and collectively we applied for water, electricity and toilet facilities. Rajobai's family did not involve themselves in these community activities and I felt deeply distressed by their behaviour.

Around this time I received a telegram from my cousin Kalubhai that Uncle Malabhai had died. At the funeral we discovered that Malabhai's family was in debt as they had become very poor. So we brought them to Ahmedabad with us. For some time they stayed with us and then when Kalubhai found work as a truck loader at the octroi post, we also found a small hut for them. Rajobai kept away from Kalubhai and his family, as she did not want to get involved in their difficulties, or help them.

Kalubhai loaded trucks from five in the morning to eight in the evening in order to bring back food for his wife and five children. We were ourselves in difficulty, so we could not help him financially. But if Adambhai's son had wished, he could have helped Kalubhai as he now had a restaurant which was doing very well. Although we were all neighbours, Rajobai and her family turned a blind eye to our plight. In fact they behaved with such arrogance that we did not even feel like talking to them about our problems or those of Kalubhai who seemed to be suffering from tuberculosis.

At that point, Dr Isapji closed down his clinic, and I found work as a driver for the founder of the Ahmedabad zoo.

For a few years, we lived peacefully, but then the communal riots spread all over Ahmedabad and houses were burnt down. Only ours stood where it was—like a miracle. In our house, there was a photograph of the famous zooman. When the crowd had come with swords and petrol bombs, we had left our house and taken refuge in Juhapura. Jagabhai had placed pictures of his gods with the photograph of the zooman which had pride of place in our house. Everyone recognized the zooman's portrait as he was a much loved personality in the city. Jagabhai followed the hooligans into the house and standing in front of both pictures pleaded with folded hands that the house belonged to him and that he worked for the zooman. The rioters argued amongst themselves for a while, as some did not believe this story. But the leader of the gang stared hard at the photographs and felt that perhaps he would make a mistake if he burnt the house. He did not want the curse of the gods on him. That day Jagabhai saved our house and we thanked Allah for having given us the courage to bear the sound of Jagabhai's buffalo scraping her bad horn against our wall.

When we all returned from the refugee camp, it was now Adambhai's family who had to sleep under the roof of the sky. I couldn't help them. Kalubhai was dead and I had to arrange for his funeral. If my mother had been alive she would have sung a funeral song which would have made everybody cry. As for me, I cannot sing, the words suffocate in my throat, and all I can do is tell you this story.

Waiting for Shibraj

Vidya

When I was born, my father was on one of his many voyages and did not know that I existed. When I was a year old he returned and taking me in his lap with great surprise, started chanting Sanskrit shlokas, which I naturally did not understand. Every time he returned home, he made me sit in his lap and chanted shlokas and dialogues, much to my pleasure.

When my brother was old enough, my father started teaching him the art of becoming a bahurupi—a master of disguises. But my brother was not learning quickly enough. Instead, I was memorizing all that my father was saying and one day I surprised him by repeating all the shlokas and dialogues that I had learnt on my own. He was so happy that he hugged me and called out to my mother saying that I should be renamed Vidya, as I had all the knowledge that he would have liked my brother to have.

Perhaps my mother did not answer him and continued doing whatever she was doing at that time—possibly accounts. Whenever my father returned home, all she seemed to do was settle old accounts and start new ones. Without looking up she must have answered, 'What is the use?'

When I was a child, I rarely saw my father, and now I hardly see my husband. I look at my son as much as I can, knowing very well that when he grows up, I will see him only once a year, just like my mother and grandmother saw their husbands and sons, concealing the pain of long lonely months in their hearts, never expressing it, never giving word to it. That was their strength and I am supposed to be the same way. My husband should never know about my moments of weakness. Too much sentiment can make a man falter on his path. His feet must remain strong at all times in order to live the life he leads.

I had seen the women of my family suffer in a thousand ways, and I had decided never to suffer like them. But when I grew up, there was no escape. I suffer in the same way.

I was intelligent but was never sent to school. In fact, none of us were sent to school as we could not afford it. All that my father earned was kept as a reserve for his long absences when Mother would need every spare paisa to keep the house running. We were always afraid that we would fall apart like our roof. Repairing it was a never-ending activity. Even to this day I always watch our roof for leaks and use all my wits in keeping it over our head. The roof must be as strong as our men's feet.

I am sure by now you are curious to know more about my husband's profession. He is not a farmer, nor a schoolteacher, a cobbler, an ironsmith, an oil presser, a tailor, or a grocer. We live in a small shack in the open land behind the octroi point in a suburb of Ahmedabad, where most people work as tradesmen or labourers and come back home in the evenings. Our's is the only house where the man of the house returns every monsoon, after many months.

He is a bahurupi—an actor who can play as many roles as he wants to. All on his own. All alone. It is a profession only reserved for men; however intelligent I may be, I can never become a bahurupi. While I was growing up I knew that my mother and I would never be the ones applying make-up. Father, brothers, husband, would be the ones using make-up and wearing saris! While most girls are taught how to wear saris by their mothers, it was my father who taught me how to wear it.

That was the element of shingar, or decoration. It was a pleasure to be allowed to watch my father when he spent hours in front of the mirror trying out new dresses and make-up. He could not see much in the nine-inch mirror, but it was enough to make the necessary changes.

In fact when Father came home in the monsoon from his tours we had two nine-inch mirrors, one that stayed in his satchel and the other that stayed on the wall at home. When he was at home he polished the mirror and emptied his bag and washed it. The clothes he took out from his bag would be crumpled and soiled; sometimes a button would be missing, or the ghahghra string would be knotted up. Mother would sit in the courtyard for hours, undoing knots and cleaning Father's artificial braids with a fine-toothed comb. Then she would repair all his clothes, while Father sat and washed them with a wooden bat. Once dry, Mother folded them neatly and pressed them under a pile of mattresses. If there was a little extra money that month, I took them down to the dhobi for ironing. That is how we prepared my father's trousseau before he left again for his march after the rains.

His homecoming also meant a time of playing with the colours in his box. The memory of the colours remains particularly painful for me. At that time, my brother was being trained to become a bahurupi. One afternoon, while we were playing, he asked me if I wanted to become a monkey. I thought it would be fun to prance around like one. So my brother made a paste with the bodraj stone, multani mitti and oil. Clad only in my underwear I plastered myself with the mixture. He then taught me to jump and make sounds like a monkey. That afternoon, Father was taking a nap, which was something precious for him, as when he travelled, he always worked in the afternoons.

My very authentic 'hup, hup' imitation of the monkey's call disturbed my father's sleep. At first he was very happy that my brother had learnt the act so well. Then he saw my long hair and realized that it was the daughter and not the son who was performing. The sight infuriated him so much that he took a stick and ran after me. He chased me around the house till he caught me and beat me. Tears streamed down my cheeks as he screamed at me saying a woman could never become a bahurupi.

Worse was to follow. My brother had not told me everything about the make-up. When Mother took me for a bath, tight-lipped, she used kerosene instead of water. As she rubbed me, I felt as if my skin was on fire. Her voice was hard when she told me, 'This will teach you a lesson, and remind you what our men suffer. Their skin burns like fire with the sun and the kerosene.'

Since then, whenever I think of the menfolk, my skin simmers with the memory of my childhood, and my eyes fill with tears. No other woman could understand this except one who is born in the family of a bahurupi. I know that I am born to be a pillar of strength for the men of my family. A woman can never become an artiste, she is the guardian of the home.

Only once did we go with Father on his tour. Then, instead of travelling with him for a year, we had to return back home in two months. Mother had become pregnant and my brother had the measles.

I remember how uncomfortable that tour had been. We went to the toilet in the open, anywhere and everywhere. Our bath was merely a few tumblers of water which we poured on ourselves while standing under a tree. Sometimes we slept in fields, and I must say I was scared of the dark and the call of the spotted owlets. In every village we had to register with the police, and when we were travelling without tickets in trains or buses, Father regaled the crowd by affecting the stance of a ticket collector. But I could never enjoy his acts, as I was always afraid that a real one would walk in at that moment and put my father in prison. There were more fears than pleasures.

We did enjoy free rides in trucks, tractors and bullock-carts though. Father sang songs and Mother appeared to be happiest at that time, as she could take care of Father, giving him lunches of hot chapattis, and helping him with the saris, braids, jewellery and washing.

The only time in those months we stayed in a regular house was when my brother had the measles. Father rented a house with all the money he had earned that season, and I was happy to be under a roof where the call of the owlets and other animals did not scare me. Even now, I prefer to stay back home and be sure that I can always find a grocer and a vaid.

The roof over my head consoles me and also reminds me of the difficult life my husband leads. Alone, he walks and sleeps under the roof of the sky. Yet, he says, he does everything for the sake of art; there is no dividing line between art and life. For him, life is art, but for me it is drudgery. I tire myself out doing so many little things for the house that at night I can fall asleep in a sleep of the dead. But I always feel my husband's presence next to me and I think—God knows where he is.

Shibraj Bhand

When one is a bahurupi the day does not matter. It passes quickly under the sun, in front of an audience, entertaining them. By nightfall I am so tired that I sleep as soon as my head touches the pillow. Perhaps the most difficult time for a bahurupi is the twilight hour, when one can sometimes see an evening star shining in the deep blue sky over a thin line of a burning red horizon. That is the time Vishnu appeared as half-lion, half-man in the open courts of Hiranyakashyapu and slayed him. He was neither man nor woman, neither animal nor bird, and it was neither day nor night. I pray to him in the altar of my mind to give me strength and inspiration.

I knead the dough for my evening bread and think of Vidya, so far away in our house, perhaps doing the same, kneading dough, or perhaps boiling some khichdi, or maybe lighting the kitchen fire and the lanterns. Darkness scares her and I always worry for her and the children. While kneading the dough I throw a lingering look at my quilt, the one that Vidya had stitched for me with the rags of her old saris. It is colourful and it always makes me think of her and feel I am sleeping next to her.

As I prepare my meal I try to decide which act I should perform the next day. I could become a tiger or a lion or perhaps be the poet-queen Mira. I like being Mira. She reminds me of Vidya in her fierce dedication to the one she loves. I always think of Mira as Vidya in a white flowing sari, an ektara in one hand, hair flowing over her left shoulder, long like the hairpiece bought from the Sunday market on the river. Perhaps the braid comes from Tirupati, where women offer their hair, or perhaps it is good old horse hair, but when I touch it, it does seem to be like a woman's hair—soft and flowing. It lies curled up in a plastic bag at the bottom of my bag, and so does the white nylon sari. The last time I was with Vidya, she had taunted me as I had not bought one for her, instead I had bought one for myself. This must be one of the strangest homes, where saris and brassieres are bought for both husband and wife!

The only problem about becoming Mira is that the make-up should be perfect. In fact, one has to work hard on all types of make-up, but to become a woman one has to rub the bodraj stone longer on the face to get the softness and roundness of feminine cheeks. The eyes should be gentle and affectionate. For this one has to practice long in front of the mirror. It takes me two hours in just trying to be a woman while it takes a woman just a glance, a gesture, or a touch.

To have the right walk is also necessary, I have to change my manly bearish walk into something that has grace, beauty, curves and flow. Besides that, the hands and legs must have a clean look, with the red alta painted on the heels and palms. There has to be a real transformation.

But then, all of us have within us male and female elements. So when I do the role of Shiva as Ardhanareshwar, I feel complete. Thinking of women and gods, I feel homesick, sad and weak. So I think about lions and tigers and my great-grandfather who always liked to play the role of a tiger. But I must confess that although I talk about the vesh of the tiger or a lion, I rarely play it. I have played a bear sometimes. But the bear's mask with a furry body-dress made of sheep hair suffocates me. I only become a bear in the winter season and entertain schoolchildren, who like such performances better than anything else.

My mind goes back to the story of the tiger. It is always good to remember these stories when one is sad.

My great-grandfather was a very good bahurupi and he had once taken the vesh of a tiger for several days. Soon word spread that a man-eater was on the prowl. So the king decided to kill him and organized a shoot. When he cornered the 'tiger' and raised his gun to shoot, my great-grandfather stood up and revealed himself. But the king had already pulled the trigger, and the bullet hit my grandfather's knee. Thereafter, he was always referred to as the lame one. The king was so pleased with the realism of the act that he gave my great-grandfather a silver rupee and fifty acres of land. Imagine, fifty acres of land!

There is no more any land. We live in a rented house and Vidya is always afraid that the roof is going to fall. The family was never around to look after the land as we were always on the move. No one from the family ever tilled the land and in the process, somebody else was the farmer. So when the land ceiling act was enforced, the farmhand became the owner. There are records in the tehsildar's office, but just to open the file, do you know how much money he wants? Five thousand rupees. Now who has seen so much money? And if I had so much money do you know what I would do? Go to Bombay!

But there are more urgent things to be decided now, like which role I shall play tomorrow. And I forget, did I register myself with the police?

Before I decide, I must eat the chapattis while they are hot, with a piece of jaggery. By the time the day is out I feel so hungry that I eat like a tiger and my mind goes back to my great-grandfather. In order to perfect his act and become an authentic tiger, he studied the animal closely. I assume he went to the forest or to a maharaja's zoo, where he sat for hours trying to match the facial structure of the tiger by blowing up his cheeks. He also got a mask made, so that the whiskers could be arranged in the right place. He learnt to sit like a tiger and walk on his fours with an effortless feline grace. For hours he walked on his fours, moving the wire in his tail with his body movement and putting the right pressure of his feet on the leaves strewn on the ground to match the stealth of the tiger. He studied the growls and snarls and in a cave he found in the forest he practised with the echo of his own growls. This rigorous training must have made him hate being a bahurupi.

But that is not all, there is always much more to a

role; like the colour of the make-up. The yellow colour of the tiger with the stripes must have taken my great-grandfather hours of meticulous painting, first rubbing the bodraj stone with water to give the desired volume to the body, and then applying the bright yellow pivdi colour. This would have been followed up with delicate brushwork. I am sure he took the help of his sons or an apprentice. Or he must have worn a tiger's body-dress, made from yellow painted cloth, which his tailor must have stitched for him.

The story always amazes me. His act was so perfect that it fooled the villagers into thinking there was a tiger on the prowl in the forest. For this he must have had to dress for hours ahead of time, and live in the forest so as to scare the villagers. I always wonder how he washed or prepared his food; how he coped with being a man and a tiger at the same time. I am sure he became a tiger in spirit for some days and forgot what it meant to be a man. He must have prowled around in his make-up and almost lived in his dress, so that people were convinced that he was a tiger.

Vidya

I am convinced that my man is a tiger amongst men. Whenever I think of him, I think that he is roaming alone in the forest of the world. Alone and bold, walking into unknown places at odd times, facing suspicious glances and checking in the police station, just in case there is a robbery. An impersonator is more suspect than any other man.

For most people he is an impersonator—he is not who he is, but somebody who transforms himself into another form.

When my husband begins his stay in a village, he always starts with playing the roles of gods. It makes him feel protected and sheltered. It is a safety measure holding the key to a welcome and fills the villagers with awe.

In my house, before night falls, I light the lantern and pray to God that my bahurupi is impersonating the Almighty, so that nobody casts an evil eye on our house. I always like to think that when he is so far away—hoping that people will only worship him, not ridicule him or insult him.

Who is a bahurupi after all? He is but an animal, a sculpture which has fallen from heaven. The story of the bahurupi is linked to the downfall of man, as mentioned in the Genesis.

When the universe was created, God first created light and then the creatures who were going to inhabit it. So, He took some clay and created man in the likeness of Himself, after which He gave him a companion by fashioning a woman from the man's rib. Paradise was their home, but God forbade them to take fruit from the tree of life. To give them more pleasure God also decorated paradise with various sculptures.

But this eden of happiness was not to last long. The devil, in the form of a serpent, tempted the woman to eat the apple from the tree of life. She took it, and offered the same to the man. God was angry that the couple had eaten from the tree of life, and expelled them from paradise. A flaming sword circled paradise and the power of God's anger was such that the idols fell down on earth and took the form of various creatures. These creatures were our ancestors—the bahurupis. That is what most of us believe about our ancestry.

Another belief is that Krishna and Shiva were the

original bahurupis who could transform themselves into any form to drive away evil forces from the face of the earth. Both gods could perform miracles in their various forms. So bahurupis take inspiration from them.

The inspiration comes in a thousand and one ways. The story of the tiger which had tried to attack Shiva must have inspired our ancestors to think of the tiger act. The story goes that a tiger had charged at Shiva, but in the split of a second, Shiva lifted the animal and threw him over his back. Immediately the animal was transformed into a pelt, and since then Shiva wore it like a garment. This is how bahurupis transform themselves into tigers, bears, monkeys, gods and so many other forms. They also weave stories and incidents from daily life, so that the audience is always entertained with themes which touch their lives.

The weight of the morning is always heavy on the bahurupi, he has to think in detail about his role, the words he will say, the dress he will wear and the type of make-up he will use. My bahurupi is very clever. Every morning when he wakes up, he prepares his dialogues. It is good that he can read and write. He writes and memorizes all that he has to say. This includes the funny stories he tells to make people laugh. In a crowd, laughter works better than anything else. The tension eases and he relaxes and says all that he has to say with a lot of courage.

Some roles can be performed easily. Like it is easy for a bahurupi to be a ticket collector on a train. Without using make-up he can easily pass off as one and travel without a ticket. But I dread the day he will encounter a real ticket collector. Yet, when my husband returns, he never tells me about his difficulties or troubles—whether he had to pay a fine, or had to get off the train and walk a long distance. Sometimes his money order does not reach me in time and I know that something has gone wrong. So I buy food on credit from the grocer and promise to pay him back as soon as I receive the money order or when my husband returns. Fortunately, so far, I have never kept the bills pending.

In many ways we are like the image of Ardhnareshwara. We are man and woman, but we take responsibility together. And although he may wear the sari as often as I do, one thing is certain—he is a man, and above all, he is a bahurupi, and I am not.

As a woman living alone my only protection is the four walls of my house and the latch on the door. Anyway, this is not a topic for discussion and it is obvious that it is necessary for the woman to stay back and look after the house, so that a large part of the family is taken care of. It may be old parents, children, brothers, sisters-in-law and sometimes perhaps a piece of land that she may have to till on her own. All this work demands superhuman strength at times.

Besides that, the children have to be sent to school. Every evening I ask my eldest to see that they do their homework regularly. I dread to think of the year when he will have to miss school and go with my husband for training. Even now it is very difficult to get him interested in studies and I have to force him to finish his homework. He prefers to jump around and act as though he were a seasoned bahurupi. If he drops out from school it will be very difficult to send him back.

Besides being a bahurupi, we also want him to study and become a sahib, because the bahurupi's art is difficult, and families remain separated for a long time.

When the work is too much I think of the story behind the Ardhnareshwara form of Shiva. It was Narad, the eternal traveller and mischief-maker, who had instigated Parvati against Shiva by telling her that Shiva was careless and supported his family by begging. Parvati became so infuriated that she wanted to walk out on Shiva. It was then that Narad realized that he had gone too far in his mischief-making and told her that Shiva also had his good points, so he advised her to arrange for the food herself instead of depending on an ascetic like Shiva. Parvati took his advice and made her own arrangements for the evening meal. When Shiva returned, he was very hungry, and the sight of food pleased him so much that he became one with Parvati. So the Ardhnareshwara is half-woman, half-man, yet joined together in body and mind; a cementing of thoughts about how to keep the house running, how to keep the art of bahurupi alive. Art which is life, because even otherwise my husband does not know what else to do.

Shibraj Bhand

Perhaps today I will take the form of Ardhnareshwara. People like it, especially women, and look on at this act as a form of worship. When it is over they sometimes offer food. It also reminds me of the responsibility I share with Vidya. This keeps me away from trouble and I do not feel attracted to other women, as I pass months without Vidya's tender touch. Yet, it is a harsh reality of my life that the distance between my mouth and hand is so long that I cannot afford another woman in my life.

This particular dress is very important for me as it is the personification of Shiva and we bahurupis take our inspiration from him and his capacity to take any disguise—from a mendicant to a thundering god performing the dance of death. He has the capacity to both create and destroy.

In any neighbourhood, village, or city, we perform for six to seven days, in the same way that God needed seven days to create the earth. I plan an act a day and keep a diary with the names of shops and the people for whom I perform. They are my patrons. At the end of the seventh day, I bow to them and tell them how I entertained them for the past few days and if they liked what they saw, they could give me any amount they felt I deserved. Most people are generous when I have revealed to them the beauty of the gods, but some sneer at me, saying, 'Well, why should I pay you? I did not ask you to come here.' These are moments of great insult. It is a degradation of my art. Whatever people think of this art, we are not beggars. At least I hate to be referred to as a beggar, just because our art demands the collection of money. It really makes me very angry. To the people who abuse my art, my answer is a deep silence because I believe in beauty and humility.

When one dresses as a god, one must forgive those who offend. But let me tell you about the dress of Ardhnareshwara. It is very complicated and tricky. First I have to divide myself—emotionally—and tell myself that one part of my body must move with the strength and virility of a man, and the other with the grace and delicacy of a woman.

A lot of planning goes into the dress and the make-up. The first time I attempted this act I made detailed sketches on the pages of my son's drawing book, then my neighbour Mangu, the tailor, and Vidya stitched it for me. It was essential that the line of the dress should exactly cut my body in two halves and there should be a perfect synchronizing of both parts.

I decided that Shiva should be bare chested with serpents coiled around his neck and that Parvati should wear a blouse and a sari with a zari border. For this we made a half-blouse in purple satin which I tied with a string around my waist and shoulder. Into this I inserted a coconut shell, to give the appearance of a breast. On my bare chest, hands and face I rubbed the bodraj to give depth and roundness. Then I slowly painted a blue colour mixed with oil on the left side on my face and my left leg, which would be visible. In this way, one half of my face had the indigo of Shiva, and the other was pink for Parvati. Around my neck I hung a snake that Vidya had made for me with rags.

On my Parvati side, I wore a bright pink sari which fell perfectly on my right leg, and around my left hip I wore a brown loincloth, as Shiva's dress. While I wore bangles and armlets on my right hand, I wore rudraksha beads on my left.

However, the most difficult part was to follow. It was the face. I first parted my hair and tied a wig which appeared like a top knot on the left side fitted with a cardboard half-moon, while a braid with red tassles was fixed on the other side. Then with great delicacy I painted a trident on the left side of the forehead and a bright red dot on the right side. I stuck bead earrings in one ear and gold tops in the other. On the left side of my lips I applied a black colour, and on the other side, to show Parvati's lips, I used red.

Then I saw myself in my nine-inch mirror. There is a limit to what one can see in a mirror of this size. Sometimes I could see only the male side of the eyes, at

nd although both eyes
n looked at from different
pride and manliness while
ty.

verall picture of my image.
ror far away from my body,
sion. At other times I place
watch myself from a distance.
e a good idea about adding
In a mirror of the same size,
r eyes with ease and knows
exactly _____ te.

Whenever I dress as Ardhnareshwara, I feel complete like the universe, and miss Vidya and the children a little less as I voice the dialogue between Shiva, Parvati and Narad, my voice ranging from the softness of a woman's murmur to the loud and gruff tones of a man. I enact the little differences between husband and wife and Narad's mischief which almost ruined their marriage. I end the skit by relating the union of the two with bawdy jokes. As I perform I believe that I am Shiva and Parvati at the same time. Moving with power and sensuality for a moment I really am half-man, half-woman and the two were never separate.

Yet I know that at night the moment of ecstasy will fall off my back like the skin of a serpent. When I will wash the oil and colour from my face, I'll know by the fire that burns through the pores of my skin that I am a man and nothing can change that, and that it will be many nights before I see Vidya and experience the fullness of our being together.

From the form of Ardhnareshwara, I have been inspired to do the act of Gora-Kala or Black and White—

the negative and positive forces of life, like night and day. But let me be honest, I saw a film of the same name at Sonal cinema near our house. It had been a rare family outing and I had been enthralled by the duplicity of the actor and memorized all the dialogues which had a lot of references to good and evil. This was a good starting point, so under the streetlight at the octroi post, I made detailed notes of the two characters and wondered how I could create one image out of the two. It was then that the gods came to my aid and in the tradition of the half-man and half-woman, I created two men in one—black and white. Like two sides of a coin.

For this role I fashioned a dress which had a black suit for the black face and a white suit for the white face. And then with a lot of practice, I created a reddish angry look in one eye and a soft sombre look in the other. Sometimes when I study the marketplace or the area around the station, I decide against playing God as the people look as if they will be more interested in filmi roles, in sensation rather than spirituality.

When I played this role for the first time I was very nervous and not sure how people would react. But that afternoon I was very lucky as with my opening dialogue, a few young people standing at a paan shop immediately made the connection with the film and I received a big applause and tips. But then word spreads fast about such roles, and I heard to my amazement that other bahurupis were also performing the same act.

Like Gora-Kala, every cloud has a silver lining and every silver lining has a dark cloud.

Vidya

I dread to think of the crowds that sometimes follow my

husband. There are times he may have taken the form of Hanuman, jumping on rooftops and trees. This sight excites children so much that they follow him wherever he goes.

When the bahurupi is dressed like a monkey, he is caught in his own trap. He knows only too well that this is the most entertaining of all roles, with the enormous tail bobbing behind his back, the mouth puffed up and coloured red making sounds of hup, hup, hup. This is enough to create a frenzy. And, believe me, a bahurupi must be very patient and wait till sundown, when all his tormentors leave him alone, so that he can go to the village well or lake or close the door of his rented room, if he has been lucky enough to find one, and untie his tail and wash the red colour from his face.

But what I am about to tell you refers to an incident that happened to my husband when he was still experimenting with the Gora-Kala act. In one particular town where the film of the same name had been very popular, the crowds of children in the streets were hysterical to see a real-life version of the man, so they followed him, screaming out in loud voices the dialogues from the film. My husband was at a loss. It was one of the rare moments of his life when he did not know what to do with the crowd. Whatever he said seemed to provoke the crowd, which was getting out of control.

As a bahurupi he has learnt that one does not speak, nor get angry during such moments. So he kept walking with the crowd following him. He told me that at one point he was afraid that the crowd would tear his clothes in their frenzy. This happens rarely to a bahurupi, but it can happen.

Then he made a mistake, although he knew that he

should not have done it. He changed his route and headed for the police station, as he felt that the police could help him. But the officer on duty quickly arrested my husband and shooed away the crowd. My husband was relieved and sat down quietly on the wooden bench, hoping that the policeman would offer him a saucer of the tea that he was drinking. But he did not. My husband spent the night in the police lock-up, as it was assumed that he was a robber who frequented the town.

He told me this story much later when he returned home, and said that he had never hated his make-up as much as he had that night.

Instead of the usual pink bodraj, he had the black and white colour dividing his face into two parts. To add to this, his make-up was such that one eye looked angry and the other sober. There was no way for him to get some kerosene and remove the paint. All he could do was wait for a saviour. He tried to tell the policeman on duty that he was not the robber but a bahurupi and had been listed with such and such policeman a week before. Somehow the man did not want to listen, and my husband knew that this was going to be an endless night. The roads on which he loved to walk seemed far away and unreachable. He realized his mistake, and felt that it was better to be chased by a crowd than spend the night in lock-up. He started feeling dizzy and could not decide which situation was better or worse.

But with morning, like the sunlight which follows the rain, another policeman replaced the first one and he recognized my husband. He released him from the lock-up room and giving him a hot cup of tea asked him to repeat a dialogue from the famous Gora-Kala role.

My husband says that it was one of his most difficult

performances. The make-up was sticky and had stayed on the face too long, he was not in a mood to be either black or white, all he wanted to be was himself. Yet freedom was more important than anything else, and he gave a small performance, much to the pleasure of the policeman.

After this incident my husband feels his role has become like an ill-omen and never performs it unless he is sure about the crowd. In fact, sometimes before dressing for Gora-Kala, he goes into the street and asks his clients if they would like to see something from the films.

As for me, I catch myself thinking many a times, I hope he is not jumping off roofs like a monkey or playing Gora-Kala.

Shibraj Bhand

Whenever I become Hanuman, I remember the difficult training that I received from Lala Bahurupi. He had the reputation of performing the most authentic monkey act of all times. He was short and had a big head with small legs but he could do the most amazing jumps that I have ever seen. Even his voice had an amazing boom which was better than any monkey call I have ever heard from other bahurupis.

My father chose him as my guru when I was fourteen years old because, he said, it is always good to train with another bahurupi at that age. That is how I came to live with Lalaji. I remember the time I spent with him as a time of both tears and small pleasures.

When Lalaji played Hanuman, it was difficult to tell him from the monkeys. He could do the most unusual jumps, backwards and forwards, and still land on his feet.

He was also very agile at jumping from one tree to another.

He started his training by telling all the stories he knew about Hanuman and the Ramayana. He told me that when Vishnu decided to descend on earth as Rama, to destroy the ten-headed demon Ravana, he is known to have told the other gods, 'From the bodies of the chief apsaras, the gandharvas, the yakshinis, the vidyadharis, the kinnaris and the female monkeys—procreate sons.' Hanuman, the son of Marut, the wind god, was wise and powerful like the thunderbolt and as swift as an eagle. To assist Rama, these monkeys appeared all over the earth. They could take any form—of man or beast. Hanuman was the most powerful of them all. His loyalty to Rama was such that it has become the epitome of faithfulness.

When Rama defeated Ravana and returned to Ayodhya, he asked Hanuman what boon he desired in reward for his great service. Hanuman asked permission to live as long as the story of Rama would be remembered. The boon was granted, and it is believed that Hanuman still lives in some inaccessible mountain in the Himalayas.

Another story is that Hanuman was born to an apsara who had been transformed into a she-monkey by a curse. It is said that she was impregnated by a rice cake which had been made by Guru Vashisht as a sacrificial offering for King Dashrath. The cakes were to be given to his three wives. Kaikeyi, who was served last as she was the youngest, did not accept it as she took this as an insult. At that very moment an eagle swooped down and carried away the cake. Flying over a mountain, it saw Anjana the apsara–monkey, and dropped the cake in her palm. At that very moment Shiva appeared before her and asked her to eat the cake. She obeyed him and conceived

Hanuman. According to yet another story, Marut is supposed to have directed the cake into Anjana's hands. Another account says that Marut ravished Anjana and pacified her by saying that a great son would be born to her.

There are many fantastic tales about Hanuman's strength. He could course through air with the swiftness of wind, assume any size, uproot trees, and make himself invisible. As a child he was forever hungry and is known to have swallowed the sun god, but had to spit him out as he burnt his mouth. Since then, Hanuman is always depicted with a red face. It is said that Hanuman flew all the way to Lanka and back, and while he was flying in the sky he saw a demon who opened her mouth to swallow him. The width of her mouth was immense, but Hanuman reduced his size and became so small that he escaped through her ear.

In Ravana's kingdom, while he was looking for Sita, he became the size of a cat. When Laxman was wounded in the great battle with Ravana, Hanuman flew to the Himalayas in search of Sanjivini—the life-giving herb. Not able to locate it, Hanuman flew an entire mountain to Laxman's rescue.

I spent a large part of the mornings sitting with Lalaji under a tree with a Ramayana between us on a wooden book holder. I learnt to recite all the important passages.

After this I would prepare a fire with twigs and make tea and chapattis for our breakfast, leaving some for lunch. Then we would sit cross-legged facing each other and Lalaji would teach me eyebrow exercises. I learnt to bring my eyebrows down over my eyes in a straight line and to stare without blinking for half an hour. This would create a white haze in front of my eyes and sometimes I would see many images of Lalaji.

Then Lalaji would ask me to puff out my cheeks for a full half an hour. In the beginning this was difficult as my mouth would fill with spittle and I would be scared of moving for fear of blowing spit in Lalaji's face, as he might then cane me. According to my father the cane was necessary for memory, as its sting sharpened the senses.

I was very happy with the result of my monkey face, the image of which Lalaji allowed me to watch in his mirror. I imagined myself to be a great bahurupi who would look like a real monkey. The exercises were always followed by a lunch of vegetables that Lalaji cooked for us, and after a short nap, our afternoons were devoted to body exercises.

But that was not enough; much more was to follow. One afternoon Lalaji asked me to stare into his eyes. He then brought down his eyebrows, and with a quick sweep of his fingers he turned his eyelids upwards, so that his eyes resembled those of a monkey.

I stared at the red veins in his eyelids. But he was calm and relaxed as he sat in the lotus pose with his hands resting on his knees, his bare chest puffed out like that of a male monkey. I sat shivering with fear in front of Lalaji, worrying about how my eyes would hurt when I did the exercise. I tried hard but I could not turn them upwards. I could see Lalaji's hands twitch on the cane. In fact at that moment he appeared to me like an enormous male monkey that was about to tear me apart.

His hand moved towards my face and I froze in anticipation of a slap. Instead, he gently turned my lids upwards. Silently, I suffered the stinging pain in my eyes, which disappeared as the tears began to flow. In the mirror that he held in front of my face, I saw my transformation into a real monkey.

In the afternoons I did exercises in order to develop my chest, biceps and thighs. Then I practised high jumps on my own. First I jumped on the ground, then from one mound to another, all the time dreading the day I would fall and break a bone. I was very careful, and learnt to fall on the flats of my feet or on my fours. According to Lalaji, minor cuts and bruises were not to be taken into consideration.

For further observation of their behaviour patterns, we followed a group of monkeys by hiding in the bushes, as they jumped from one tree to another. At the end of the day we returned to Lalaji's house in the village, where we cooked hot khichdi and vegetables. I always looked forward to these quiet evenings when I could bathe under a tap and sleep peacefully. But then, if everything is peaceful, it cannot be a bahurupi's life.

So far I had learnt the basics, and in a month I was ready for what Lalaji called a hunt. In this we had to lie low in the bushes and watch the monkeys, following them as they moved from one tree to another. This was not necessary for the Hanuman act, but Lalaji wanted me to understand the spirit of a monkey, so that the body could react with authenticity.

Lalaji sat on his haunches in the bushes and imitated the monkeys by scratching and picking nits. I did the same. Then slowly we came out of the bushes in full view of what appeared to be a friendly monkey family. In yet another week, the monkeys had got accustomed to us and Lalaji fed them with chapattis and groundnuts. I did not realize what Lalaji's aim was till he asked me to climb the tree and stay there for the day.

This was the most scary part of the training. But once

I was on the tree there was no turning back. I had to survive the whole day with the monkeys. Yet Lalaji was kind and had fed me very well in the morning. He was always there, hiding in the bushes and watching me.

On the first day, the male monkey who was the head of the family, fixed me with an unblinking stare and then grimaced, showing me all his teeth. I sat still with my mouth blown up and eyebrows slanting over my eyes. I sat frigid till he had turned his back on me and I knew that I was accepted in his troupe.

All day long, I jumped and swung on branches with my fellow monkeys. In a week Lalaji had reason to be proud of me as I was picking nits from the ears of the younger monkeys who also inspected mine. I had also learnt to jump from one tree to another. It wasn't entirely smooth going, however. One day two young males got into a fight with me, and I was afraid that they would scratch my eyes out, so all I could do as an act of defeat was ward off their attacks and jump to another tree. Lalaji had warned me that I should never get bitten by a monkey or else I would have to be rushed for injections to the hospital, which was very far away.

When I warded off the young monkeys, Lalaji cheered me with his thumb in the air and smiled for the first time since I had accepted him as my guru. I was pleased, but my pleasure turned to horror as the next day Lalaji told me to eat well for I had to spend two nights with the troupe of monkeys. I was alarmed but did not show my fear to Lalaji. When he returned to the village without looking back, I felt like clinging to him like a baby monkey.

That evening as I sat on a tree, watching a golden sunset, I was so frightened that I did not even feel hungry. I shuddered as I heard the wing beats of bats and owls in the stillness of the night. The monkeys were sleeping close to each other and soundlessly I started crying. Then I dozed off, and felt warm as one of the younger monkeys had cuddled up to me.

When I had passed this test of fire, Lalaji taught me the art of make-up, by colouring the face either as the black-faced langur or the red-faced monkey. But Hanuman had to always have a red face. He also taught me to stick sheep hair on the beard and eyebrows, to paint the body grey, and to make a tail with wire and rags. He showed me how to make a crown, armlets and mace—the accessories I would need for my Hanuman dress.

Now, whenever I play Hanuman, I know Lalaji's spirit is with me and that there is nothing to fear as I jump from one tree to another.

Vidya

As I watch my young son playing marbles with the boys in the street, my heart aches for him. Next year he will be out on the roads as an apprentice to his father. That is the fate of all bahurupi boys. I feel sorry for my son, as now he goes to school, but once he takes to the road with his father, he will find it difficult to go back to his studies. But I have insisted that he will have to do both—continue with his studies and also learn how to be a bahurupi. He has to continue the tradition and yet have some basic education. It is a hard life for a boy to be on the road, sometimes without food and water, till they reach a friendly village or town.

Fortunately my son, Keshav, does not have to suffer as much as my husband did as a teenager. It is an understanding between us that he will initially only carry bags, prepare costumes, help with the make-up, learn to cook, fill water, wash clothes, learn everything about villages, towns and cities, and generally watch how his father works.

And on some days, instead of his father he will play Krishna in a pitamber, with kohl in his eyes, a peacock feather in his crown and a flute on his lips. For me this image of him as the blue god will stay in my mind, and I will not think how uncomfortable he will be on the road. Perhaps he will be all right, he is after all the son of a bahurupi. But I shall miss him as much as I miss my husband.

Today I am sure my husband is in some town or village dressed as Narad and entertaining people. Narad is a lovable and mischievous character. For this role a bahurupi must be able to involve the audience in a witty dialogue. My father-in-law had seen the film *Sati Anasuya* and had fashioned himself on the actor who had played Narad, complete with the dialogues which had become very popular in those days. He had then taught the same to my husband, who had added his own touches to the role.

I can see him smiling and standing before me in his yellow dhoti and shawl, with a veena in his hands, beads around his neck, flowers in his braid and a pink glow on his face. Narad is very popular with villagers because he always seems to be in dialogue with an imaginary god. Basically he is very mischievous, and is known to move easily in all the regions of heaven and earth, where he disrupts the lives of both gods and human beings. To create discord is his profession, so his language is very provocative. Yet he is not a bad person, as at the end he mends all the quarrels and conflicts that he may have created.

Once when there was peace on heaven and earth, it was the perfect timing for Narad to create discord. He told Parvati that Anasuya, the wife of a rishi, was more beautiful than her. He repeated the same to Saraswati and Laxmi. The three goddesses were furious, and asked their husbands to tempt Anasuya as she was very faithful to her husband. The three gods—Brahma, Vishnu and Shiva—decided to act together. When they reached Anasuya's house as mendicants, she offered them food. They seated themselves and demanded that Anasuya serve them in the nude. Hearing this Anasuya washed her husband's feet, took the water and sprinkled it on the three gods and transformed them into little children.

The gods were now trapped in a cradle, and could not regain their original forms. They were compelled to live as Anasuya's children, till the goddesses implored her to release their husbands. Anasuya agreed on the condition that the goddesses create the three-headed divinity Dattatreya for her. Only then would she return their husbands to them.

Narad is the creator of suspicion and I wonder whether he will also play tricks with my family. Once at midnight, I heard a strange hiss in the corner of our one-roomed house. I collected the children together and saw that there was a snake in the house.

In a panic I banged on the door of my neighbour Kishorebhai's house, who swiftly killed it with a stick. When we thanked him with folded hands, I noticed he gave me a long look and I, too, looked at him and thought that it would have been so nice if he had slept in our house that night. All night long I lay awake and missed my husband. I did not even know where he was. I tortured myself with the doubt as to whether he would ever be unfaithful to me. My mother had taught me that one had to be prepared for occasional lapses of faith, as the men stayed alone for long periods and sometimes when they had extra money they spent it on a woman. But that, according to her, is never often, as a bahurupi is brought up with a strong sense of responsibility for his family and is always aware of their dependence on him for everything. In many ways a bahurupi is like the celibate Narad—capable of flowery language, but who keeps away from lust and anger.

Shibraj Bhand

Next year, when I travel, my son will be with me. This will keep me from getting distracted, like the time I was attracted to a young woman in the audience. I was playing Narad and knew that I was looking very handsome with the topknot and the flowers in my braid. My skin was shining like pink pearls and she was staring at me entranced. She must have been about twenty. She had a warm brown face and narrow almond eyes. There was oil in her hair, with a yellow flower tucked in casually. The green and red sari with the yellow blouse accentuated her charm. In fact she lookes like Vidya to me, or perhaps I was missing my wife so much that every beautiful woman resembled her.

I could have easily caught her eye and made some appreciative comment about her looks, because a bahurupi has an artist's license. But then, an artist's eye is also observant, and I saw that she had turned her head away, and was speaking to a man. When I saw the man, I heard the bell of caution ringing in my head. His skin betrayed him. He was also a bahurupi. Our skin drinks so much kerosene, that it betrays our profession. His eyes were bright and analytical as he watched me. So I underplayed my role. I did not want to give away my best lines, as bahurupis tend to imitate each other, and jealousy between artistes is a common trait.

When I ended my act, the man came forward and introduced himself as Daud Bhand. To my surprise he congratulated me and said that he had never seen a better Narad. I kept my eyes averted from the girl and hoped that Daud had not seen my interest in her, as it was obvious that she was his wife. They invited me to their house for dinner, saying that they knew how difficult it is for a bahurupi to eat dry chapattis day after day. That night, as I slept on a mattress in their house, I felt a sense of warmth and well-being. It was like meeting old friends after a long time. And I thanked god that I had averted my eyes from Daud's wife, as Narad could have easily played a trick on me.

So, the presence of my son will keep me alert about my responsibilities. It will be good to dress him as a child Krishna as it immediately catches the interest of the audience, specially women, and sometimes a child Krishna earns much more than an adult bahurupi.

The training will make him hardy, as he will learn to walk miles, travel without a ticket or hitch rides in tempos or trucks. His legs will ache and he will always be tired, but then, that will be his basic training—to keep on going. And we will protect each other.

As we travel, I will teach him how to create a divine atmosphere with words. In the process he will learn all about designing costumes and jewellery. Then he will learn the technique of make-up and basic tailoring. He will learn how to utilize one clothing for many acts. I know he will be bored with making chapattis, as Vidya pampers him and he is used to eating them hot, straight from the griddle. I will teach him to light a fire with dry twigs and prepare the evening meal.

But at night, sleeping in the same quilt, I will teach him to tell directions by the position of the stars and planets. He will learn to identify birds, animals and reptiles, and also understand human beings. This will help him anticipate danger. Most bahurupis carry their own cash for days till they reach a post office, so he will have to learn the various methods of hiding money and carrying all his belongings in just one bag. All these experiences will make him fearless.

Besides these mundane activities, every morning he will prepare dialogues and scripts for his own act and mine; he will also learn to develop an instinct for a town, village or city—to determine what sort of roles would be popular and how much he could earn there. He will learn to sense situations with his eyes, ears and instincts. He will help in tying knots, adjusting wigs and changing clothes. But the most enjoyable aspect of our being together will be the narration of all my acts.

Vidya worries too much about education, but this is also an education. I will teach him all the languages I speak. No school can teach him what he will learn from me. Eventually, when he returns to school, he will definitely know much more about life. But Vidya has a point when she says that he will lose interest in school, because this is the price Keshav has to pay for being born a bahurupi.

At the end of the training he will have learnt the meaning of the old bahurupi saying—*Ek noor aadmi, Hazaar noor kapda, Hazar noor taap teep, Lakh noor nakhra* (The aura of every human being multiplies in thousands with the right clothes, make-up and jewellery. But the right mannerism helps the aura multiply in lakhs.) The essence of a bahurupi is his intellect, his make-up, the thousand and one costumes, all shining with the nuances of his acting abilities. Once he perfects these, he will feel like a king and not a beggar, when at the end of the seven days of playing various roles he will collect money.

People sometimes think of us as beggars and I will teach my son never to enact a beggar's role on the last day and never to accept money while dressed like a beggar. These are some rules one must follow in order to retain the dignity of an artiste. However, to earn is also the right of an artiste. How else can we survive? I must tell my son to beware of playing a beggar or a madman as with a wrong word or action the audience can beat us and hound us like dogs. He must develop good eye contact with his spectators, like I had learnt to develop with the big male monkey.

As the child Krishna he can accept money which people give with love and devotion. Krishna, after all, is the one who initiated the art of bahurup. It is said that Krishna learnt the sixty-four arts and fourteen studies from the sage Sandipani. We consider both Shiva and Krishna as our gurus, and Kali as the mother of this art. We pay our respects to her by dressing up like her. She gives us the shakti or power to face life.

Vidya

The morning after Kishorebhai had killed the snake, he passed by to ask me if all was well. As I covered my head and offered him a cup of tea, I was trembling with fear. I hoped he had not read anything in my eyes at night. In the bright light of the sun I did not feel the same. He had a pockmarked face, and a fat body. He did not have the muscular build of my husband.

I was relieved when he continued to talk about the snake and how he had burnt it in ghee, as otherwise its mate would have come searching for it in our house. The eyes of dead snakes, he said, retain the images of past happenings. Then he said it must be difficult for us to live alone, as his friend Shibraj was away for so long, and that he would be pleased to lend his electricity line to us for half the rent. We could pay whenever Shibraj came back. This suited us well. At that moment I was the head of the family and had to take a decision, and I agreed, because we did need electricity. But I was afraid that my husband would suspect that Kishorebhai was trying to seduce me. Living alone, I was always worried that every man besides my husband was Ravana and if I ever crossed the threshold of my home, my world would be destroyed like Sita's. Then I convinced myself that Kishorebhai and his wife Sarlaben were kind to us, and that there was no hidden message in the electric line which would join both the houses.

Basically my husband is a kind man, yet whenever he plays Ravana, the demon king of Lanka, he looks as though he could kill a man with his bare hands. He knows all the legends around Ravana, such as whenever he appeared, the sun lost its force, the winds ceased to blow, the waves of the rolling oceans rose high; he had ten faces, twenty arms, copper-coloured eyes, a huge chest, and white teeth like the young moon. His strength was such that he could agitate the seas and split open the tops of mountains. Tall as a mountain peak, he could stop the sun and the moon in their courses and prevent them from rising. He terrorized gods and men, as he had received special boons from Brahma and Shiva.

Yet he was an evil demon, and Vishnu came down to earth from the heavens in his incarnation as Rama to destroy him. Ravana had given enough reason for his annihilation, as besides other evil deeds, he had carried away Rama's wife, Sita, to Lanka after tempting her to cross the Laxmanrekha. So I am always very careful when I speak to any man. I cover half my face with my sari, and keep my eyes averted.

Thinking about Ravana, I remember how we had prepared the dress when my husband had wanted to play the role. You won't believe this, but my husband is a very good painter. I suppose if he decides to stop being a bahurupi, he could always become a painter of cinema hoardings. Whenever a new act is conceived, he draws it in my son's sketch book, and decides on a general colour scheme.

For Ravana, his many heads are the most important part of the dress. So my husband borrowed some thin cardboard boxes from the grocer and made cut-outs of heads and crowns. Then he boiled earth colours with glue, placed them in different plates and sat down under a tree to patiently paint the faces with fierce expressions and big curved moustaches which almost touched the big staring eyes. Then he found another piece of cardboard and made a sword which he covered with golden paper. He did the same for the crown and then painted it with different colours. I must say it looked like a jewelled crown.

He pasted the heads in pairs of fives and fours and tied them with bamboo strips and strings on each side of his own face, so he appeared to have ten heads in all. Believe me, even when he is not playing Ravana, a bahurupi must have ten heads to create all his acts.

Yet, his jharokha is the one I like best. The balcony is very original, and he uses it for two acts. In one role he plays the single nayika or Radha waiting for her beloved, and if he has two apprentices he plays the adult Krishna with Radha and Rukmini on either side. In this act, my husband dresses like the blue god with the peacock feather in his crown and the boys are dressed as women. Sometimes, when he has enough money, he hires young boys to play the female roles.

The making of the balcony is complicated and needs a lot of planning and help. It is made by tying a printed blue cloth on a structure of bamboo strips, to give it the appearance of three walls and a ceiling. This structure is tied around his waist. But before that, he wears a pink sari with an artificial gold border and his face shines with the paste of the bodraj stone. Then with red lipstick, kohl in the eyes, a shining dot on his forehead and some artificial jewellery on his forehead, he looks just like the painting of a nayika waiting on the balcony for her lover—the way I stand in our doorway and wait for him day after day.

Shibraj Bhand

The more I think of my son, the more I worry. I wonder why. This is not the sort of anxiety that Vidya feels for him. Mine is related to his safety. I keep wondering why I am plagued with this thought.

One reason could have something to do with my brother, who was as young as Keshav when he took to the road with me. We made a mistake one day, and it was our faith in Sri Krishna which saved us. When I am out with Keshav, I must not make that mistake again. Keshav is young and innocent and should not suffer because of me.

When I was a teenager and had travelled all over India as apprentice to my father, he sent me with my little brother on a tour of five villages which were not very far from Ahmedabad. He told me to return back on a certain day. He was worried about our safety, so he stayed back and waited for my return. He reassured me that if we did not return on the day that he had decided, he would send out a search party for us.

That particular journey had become dangerous for Mohun, and he was so scared that on our return he told my father that he would prefer to go back to school rather than become a bahurupi. He did, and now he is a schoolteacher in a village not far from where we live.

Whenever I return home during the monsoons, I stop by to meet him and stay with him for some days. He lives a steady life with a regular income and sends all his children to school. But he has trained them to act, and he himself holds a small show in his school once a month, dressed either as Kali, with her black colour, string of skulls, and a red tongue, or Hanuman with his long tail, or Narad with his veena. Sometimes, if he has seen a good film, he even enacts that role. The last time I stayed with him, he imitated Manoj Kumar in the film *Kranti* to teach the schoolchildren about the freedom struggle. I was very impressed and took his permission to copy the act.

Mohun could have been an excellent bahurupi as he has a deep voice and strong body, and the filmi roles suit him very well. For *Kranti*, he powdered his hair grey and stuck a beard, also grey, on his face. He wore a white dhoti with a black coat, a red scarf and carried a wooden yoke over his shoulders to which his wrists were chained, just as in the film. But the best part was the dialogue. He narrated the tortures suffered by freedom fighters so eloquently it brought tears to my eyes.

Whenever I stay with Mohun for a week or four days, he goes through my bag and chooses to dress either as Mira, Shiva or Guru-Chela, and amuses his family and neighbours with an act in which we both participate. It is then that we are in perfect harmony and I always look forward to my stay with him.

A bahurupi by birth, he has not forgotten our tradition and loves this art. But he does not like the hazards one has to face to practise it. I know he loves to play the Guru-Chela role because he has decided to become a teacher. Invariably, he pulls out all the clothes that the role needs and although he can create the dialogue of both on his own, he prefers that I answer like a chela, while he lectures like a guru.

The costume for this act is very complicated, because one man has to impersonate two people. The guru wears a white wig and beard with a white kurta, black jacket and a colourful scarf, and his right hand rests on the chela's head, as though he were giving a blessing, while the other hand holds a stick.

The puppet-head of the chela is tied to the bahurupi's chest, so it gives the appearance that he is bent over with the burden of carrying the guru. My tailor had designed my costume with such expertise that it appears as though the student is dressed in saffron, while the guru is dressed in white.

When I am alone, I speak the dialogue of both the guru and the chela in different tones. But when I am with my brother I speak as the chela, entreating him to get off my back, but the guru will not, as I have no answers to his questions.

But jokes apart, when we part, we embrace and cry. My brother feels sorry for the sort of life I have chosen to live and fills my bag with gifts for Vidya and the children. I am happy that he has a more settled life than mine. When I turn to leave, I always feel I am the chela— bent over with the burden of my brother, the guru—for that little incident that happened when we were just boys.

As bahurupis, we have to follow certain rules, and if by chance we break one of these, we can be in deep trouble. This is exactly what happened. While travelling from one place to another, we must never perform. And, if we do, we must make sure that the role is of a sadhu, a ticket collector or a policeman. For this, one must wear old torn shoes and a bahurupi badge, so that in case a real policeman stops us, there is evidence about our identity.

But then, in those days, I was young and successful. The applause of the crowd and the sound of coins in my pocket had gone to my head, so I forgot all the rules and regulations taught by my father. Mohun was very young, good looking, fair, without a trace of hair on his face, so we decided to play a newly-wed couple. I dressed as a young man, complete with a red turban, white angarkha, dhoti and mojdis. I dressed Mohun in a deep red and blue printed choli and a lemon yellow laheriya sari which rippled on him like the golden sands of the desert. His skin glowed with the pink skin tone and he looked beautiful with lipstick and a green dot on his forehead. Then, to ward off the evil eye, I had specially painted a beauty spot on his right cheek. Nobody could have guessed that he was a boy. To give his body the right curves I had tied rags on his breasts, so that they looked small, rounded and firm. I had exposed one breast just a little to seduce the audience . . . and we were a success.

Normally, after an act we wash and wear our everyday shirts and trousers. But, on that particular day, we were to travel on foot to another town and we were in a boisterous mood with no elders around to reprimand us. In our zest, we continued walking as man and wife, without thinking about the consequences. When he reached the outskirts of a town, my brother felt the call of nature. But he was dressed as a woman, so he attended to his need like a woman, by lifting his sari and squatting on the ground. I kept on walking, assuming that he would follow me as soon as he was through.

After fifteen minutes, I suddenly realized that I could not hear the jingle of his anklets. I looked around and felt a chill when I did not see him. Immediately, I ran back to look for him.

When I reached the spot where I had left him, I found that he was warding off a policeman who was trying to molest him. Mohun was trying to tell him that he was a boy and a bahurupi at that. But the man would not desist, till I pounced on him and saved Mohun.

The policeman was now suspicious and doubted our identity. He wanted to know whether we had registered at the local police station, or else he would put us behind bars. I showed him the court affidavit with the stamp of the notary, which said 'I, Shibraj Bhand, by caste Bahurupi, of Gupta Nagar slums of city Ahmedabad, hereby proclaim that I am registered by the undersigned notary as a street actor and I have performed in various cities of India, but am mainly stationed in Ahmedabad city.' Dated such and such, with the seal and signature of the Ahmedabad courts on a stamp paper of rupees eleven.

But the policeman's ego was hurt, and he did not want to admit that he had been chasing a young boy. So he said it was a forged document, and kept on eyeing Mohun lustily. He could not believe that Mohun was not a young woman.

By then, we had realized our mistake of being dressed as a couple and did not know how to prove our credibility. He told us to follow him to the police station and started questioning us. When I insisted that Mohun was my brother, the irate policeman showered me with blows till I fell down.

I was in deep pain, yet I was thinking that the elders had a definite reason for never allowing women to become professional bahurupis. At the back of their minds, all the elder bahurupis knew that in this particular profession, the honour of women would always be at stake.

Mohun was in a state of deep shock. He did not know what to do. So, to save me he offered to show his sex, as a proof that he was a boy. I kept screaming at him not to do something as shameful as that, but he was so shattered by my condition that he had no other way. Mohun's action shocked the policeman, and he let us go without a word.

As soon as we were released, the first thing we did was to find the village well and change our clothes. We were so relieved that we held on to each other and could not stop crying. This taught me a lesson that once a bahurupi finishes his act, he must wash off his make-up and wear his normal clothes immediately—and then proceed to wherever he wants to go. Since then I never play the role of a newly-wed couple.

Mohun was too shaken to continue with the tour and

we returned home on the pretext that he had become very sick on the journey and we had to cut short our tour. If we had told our father the truth, I would have received a spanking worse than the beating I got from the policeman. The secret lies buried between both of us.

Once I reach home, perhaps I will teach Keshav all the techniques about the art of being a bahurupi. But I will not make him my apprentice. Once he has learnt the finer points, he can always use the skill to earn a little extra. And Vidya will be pleased with my decision, as Keshav is good at studies, and one day, perhaps, he will become a government servant or a schoolteacher like Mohun.

Vidya

Since early morning the crow had cawed thrice in my courtyard—a sure sign of my husband's return. I sang as I oiled my hair, and went out to buy groceries dressed in my best sari. So much so that the grocer's wife asked me if my husband had returned. All day long I cooked, arranged my hair in a different hairstyle, applied kohl to my eyes and felt like a kite flying in the sky. By evening, when he did not come, I felt depressed, deflated and stupid—how could I depend on the cawing of a crow for the return of my husband?

In fact, his return is always like a bolt of lightning on a hot summer day. He comes when he is least expected and more likely when I have nothing to offer him in the house.

For years, it has been a joke between us that one day when he returns, I will not recognize him. To this I always have a standard answer—how can a flower not recognize its own fragrance. Sometimes he is dressed as a dacoit with an eyepatch, or wears the body-suit of a bear, at other times he has returned in the garb of a demon, bearded and covered in a dress made of feathers. Or even as a modern woman in a sari—but I always recognize him by his torn shoes.

That summer the heat was unbearable, and I was worrying about my husband. He was susceptible to heat strokes and there would be nobody to look after him. He would suffer all alone. Sometimes, he would pay a young boy or an old widow to prepare bottles of nimbu-paani with lots of salt and sugar, or a sherbet of raw mangoes for him.

This summer I bought from Kishorebhai a second-hand radio as a gift for my husband and an old table fan for the house. Whenever I turn it on I feel guilty. I know that my husband must be on the road, and the heat must be burning into his feet through his worn tennis shoes, which he wears all the time.

His shoes last long, and every time there is a tear or a hole, he gets them stitched at the cobbler's, so now there are many marks which show the sewing and the patches. His shoes are a testimony to the life he leads. I taunt him about his shoes, but he never buys himself a new pair on the pretext that there are other priorities. I know he has a deep attachment for his shoes which have now become so comfortable that they are like a part of his body.

With these thoughts running through my brain, I was taking a nap one afternoon with the fan switched on at full speed when I heard a strange sound alongside that of the koel in the courtyard and the rumble of the first monsoon rain. Instinctively I sat up, worried that yet another snake had entered the house. As my eyes moved around the room nothing but the strange sound continued. I sat frozen with fear, words stuck in my throat, not even able to call out to Sarlaben. In any case, I remembered, they had gone to attend a wedding.

I was alone in the house and the afternoons in our area are quiet. The women rest indoors with their little children and teenaged daughters while the other children are still at school and the men are at work. The only person who takes a nap is the grocer, while the tailor, the barber, the cobbler, the ironsmith, the carpenter and the potter all work at their various trades all day long, so the streets around my house are deserted.

As I lifted my hand to tighten the knot of my hair, I saw the face of a madman staring down at me from a hole in the roof. I was transfixed with fear as I watched him. I felt angry with the mason who had taken a sizeable amount from me just to fix the hole. I felt alone, afraid, and missed the presence of my husband. I did not know how I was going to handle this calamity which was about to fall on my head. My first instinct was to look at the door which I had latched from inside. I knew, if I wanted to save myself, I should first run to the door and open it. I thought it would be easy, as the man was still staring at me from the roof and my first thought was of rape and murder. I could feel the sobs rising in my throat at the thought of my children, and the scene they would have to face once they returned home. In my mind's eye I could see them crying over my corpse. Looking at the crazed eyes of the man, I could only think of death.

So I clenched my fists and swiftly ran to the door. But I was late. Even before my hands could reach for the latch, the man had jumped from the ceiling and was standing between me and the door.

Now there was nothing I could do but fight him. The crazed man first went for my sari, and I had to hold on to it. It was an old sari and easily tore to shreds as I fought his hands which tried to touch my body. I was in a terrible state of shock and fear, so I opened my mouth to scream. But, before I could, he closed my mouth with his filthy hands. My eyes were dilated with fear as I watched the madman, his eyes red with anger, breathing hard, spittle running down his lips, an unbearable stink emnating from his tattered clothes.

I was helpless and at the mercy of a maniac. I was praying to Krishna, Hanuman and Shiva together, and hoping that they would come to my rescue in some form or other. But they did not, so with all the force that I could collect, I freed myself from the man's grasp and started running around the room.

He chased me, and in the process we upset everything in the house from the fan to the tin of flour, to vegetables, pots and pans, clothes, quilts, and our one and only chair. Suddenly I remembered the huge knife that my husband had given me as a precaution against thieves. I always hid it on the shelf over the stove. In a quick movement I grabbed it and stood facing the crazy man. If he took one more step towards me, I would have plunged it into his heart.

My hair was open and my face was red with the kumkum from my forehead which had spread all over with the perspiration. My eyes were wide with anger, and I could feel myself shivering as though I was in a trance. The man did not move as I must have looked like Shakti, the goddess who killed the demon.

At that moment, I heard a familiar laugh. But I was in such a state that I could not locate it. Was it coming

from the man or the roof? Or was it Narad laughing at
me? I did not want to shift my eyes from those of the
maniac. Then, slowly, I saw a transformation in the eyes
of the man. They seemed to be softening with a familiar
glint which I knew so well. I was looking into the eyes
of my husband—the bahurupi—Shibraj Bhand.

READ MORE IN PENGUIN

In every corner of the world, on every subject under the sun, Penguin represents quality and variety—the very best in publishing today.

For complete information about books available from Penguin—including Puffins, Penguin Classics and Arkana—and how to order them, write to us at the appropriate address below. Please note that for copyright reasons the selection of books varies from country to country.

In India: Please write to *Penguin Books India Pvt. Ltd. 11 Community Centre, Panchsheel Park, New Delhi 110017*

In the United Kingdom: Please write to *Dept JC, Penguin Books Ltd. Bath Road, Harmondsworth, West Drayton, Middlesex, UB7 ODA. UK*

In the United States: Please write to *Penguin Putnam Inc., 375 Hudson Street, New York, NY 10014*

In Canada: Please write to *Penguin Books Canada Ltd. 10 Alcorn Avenue, Suite 300, Toronto, Ontario M4V 3B2*

In Australia: Please write to *Penguin Books Australia Ltd. 487, Maroondah Highway, Ring Wood, Victoria 3134*

In New Zealand: Please write to *Penguin Books (NZ) Ltd. Private Bag, Takapuna, Auckland 9*

In the Netherlands: Please write to *Penguin Books Netherlands B.V., Keizersgracht 231 NL-1016 DV Amsterdom*

In Germany : Please write to *Penguin Books Deutschland GmbH, Metzlerstrasse 26, 60595 Frankfurt am Main, Germany*

In Spain: Please write to *Penguin Books S.A., Bravo Murillo, 19-1'B, E-28015 Madrid, Spain*

In Italy: Please write to *Penguin Italia s.r.l., Via Felice Casati 20, I-20104 Milano*

In France: Please write to *Penguin France S.A., 17 rue Lejeune, F-31000 Toulouse*

In Japan: Please write to *Penguin Books Japan. Ishikiribashi Building, 2-5-4, Suido, Tokyo 112*

In Greece: Please write to *Penguin Hellas Ltd, dimocritou 3, GR-106 71 Athens*

In South Africa: Please write to *Longman Penguin Books Southern Africa (Pty) Ltd, Private Bag X08, Bertsham 2013*